# Curriculum Vitae

*A.B. Boyd*

ISBN-13: 9780615790695
ISBN-10: 0615790690

Library of Congress Control Number: 2013920049
Curriculum Vitae, Los Angeles, CA

*To*
*Rabiab*

# ONE

"Forty four," Ian Sloan addressed the crack in the passenger side of the windshield which, since he rarely had a passenger and had convinced himself it was barely noticeable, remained in place. He carried a high deductible.

"Forty four." A life in numbers. Pointed. Middle age? Ridiculous. Nobody he knew reached eighty eight. His father certainly wouldn't.

"Don't stop on me you sonofabitch!" He downshifted the Rabbit as he approached the bridge. Where the hell was German precision when this wreck came off the line. "Don't stall!" Oh, sure, fine enough on straightaways, autobahn efficient, Franz and company could feel proud, but of late anything even resembling a turn and Frankenstein took control. Initially, sharp turns only, right or left, it wasn't partial, but now even a bend in the road had become a minor Armageddon.

He survived the curve and took a sip of lukewarm coffee from the mug balanced between the seats. The splatter of dark stains that riddled the floormats, Colombian, Brazilian, Sumatran - Sloan was an equal opportunity slob - had evolved into an elaborate pattern that reflected his indifference to basic maintenance and might, he felt, under the right scrutiny, yield an array of psychological insights.

A damp, sooty winter grayness hung over the arroyo. Lonely weather. He could have taken the freeway, which ran parallel not a hundred yards away, traffic hurtling past at seventy plus as he staggered along at 25mph by law, but preferred the bridge, Suicide Bridge so called for the wealthy Pasadenans who had leapt to their deaths following the '29 crash, or so legend had it, and legends appealed to Ian Sloan.

He savored the daily interlude, both going and returning, suspended on the narrow, two-lane span between ornate concrete railings and solitary lamps. And though he had never been to Europe, on sunny mornings, the marine layer not having penetrated the basin, he was transported by the early light that bathed the boarded up cliffside dwellings with their tattered balconies, beauty in disrepair, to hilltop villages, narrow, cobbled passageways climbing to open shutters, wrought iron and flower boxes...grand vistas, fluttering sails on a shimmering, azure bay...beautiful young women in summer dresses, legs crossed at sidewalk cafes, cigarette held just so, seductive lips, expectant, playful eyes...Cost Plus posters, he realized. So much for imagination.

The newly widened freeway had relegated the span to further antiquity, even less traveled, dinosauric, on the verge of extinction. Whenever a quake, major or minor, rocked the valley, it was closed for inspection. A few days, a few weeks even, as it had after the Sylmar and more recently the Whittier quake, while engineers pored over its frame, poking, prodding, as skeptics are wont to do. Any defect would suffice, but none was ever found, and the bridge inevitably reopened.

From time to time he considered the possibility, as he did again now, that the big one might strike as he approached the midway point, the concrete snapping and breaking and crumbling, plunging him and the Rabbit, a fitting end to the nemesis, headlong into the ravine. Yet he remained undeterred; indeed, of late, an early exit held a certain appeal, a 1987 high dive of sorts.

"Forty four," he repeated as he swung off the bridge. Mid life. Solidity. Prosperity. For him, simply matching digits. Bookends: too old to engage; too young to sever. Melodramatic? Maudlin? Self-absorbed? All of the above. Truth had value, he reminded himself and turned on the radio.

"Waverly Toyota time is 7:35 exactamant. A good Southern California morning." He accelerated. Only twenty minutes "Basement time, Allen. Who do you have from the nether world?"

"Whom," said Sloan.

"Max, we've got a real classic. Anne Murray. Big hit for the Canadian. Title fits – 'Snowbird.'"

No basements in LA, he noted, accelerating through the yellow light at Finch and Butler. But in Canada, Anne Murray country, his country....they had built their own.

"'Don't worry, Dad. Don't worry. I'll get my friend Paul to help. We can spread it fast.' That's what you said, damnits.'"

A spring day, overcast, a vast, gray awning of sky, the cement truck hovering above them.

"'We can spread it fast.' Spread it bloody fast all right and here I am all by my bloody self and him ready to pour and no bloody Ian...the rain coming. Jesus boy-oh-boy...bloody guttersnipe."

His friend was not home and Pete, fascinated by his footprints, was more hindrance than help. So it was left to the two of them, pushing and pulling at the ever thickening mass, a relentless flow down the chute, the inexorable, turning cylinder giving no respite, discharging its load. Ponderous gobs gathering about their rubber boots as they struggled to spread the cement across the earthen floor, the old man, having already missed his tea, slogging away in his undershirt, labored breathing, wheezing, strained curses under his breath, the driver above, arms folded, enjoying the show.

But then…But then…"Son, if you could come by sometime…If you get the chance…bloody depressing here."

"Waverly Toyota time is 7:42 and counting." Thirteen minutes. That's why they had the five minute bell, for teachers like him. Hell, he'd be lucky to make it by five after. Down Cedar and if he could catch the light at Nadine….around the corner and…don' t quit on me goddamn it. Don't…"

"Mr. Sloan, you're late."

"Thank you, Mary." Key in one hand, thermos in the other, his books and the *Times* balanced in the crook of his arm, he struggled with the lock. No attaché case for him. Affectation. Fine for business types, not teachers, not him. Most of the male staff carried them, no doubt stuffed with the same papers, taken home day after day with the best of intentions.

Ian Sloan never wanted for an opinion. Views on both the significant and the less so, a closet full of minor prejudices, rootless, trivial notions, petty biases kept hidden, but secretly acknowledged. And at the moment he considered this gaggle of disjointed adolescents a malevolent crowd gathered simply to enjoy his discomfort. In an earlier time they would have had the best seats at the Sunday hangings and provided the rope if necessary.

"Don't give me any help now. Don't disturb yourselves." His sarcasm went unacknowledged, as it usually did, except for a few. A flaw, not conducive to learning, still, part of his dark wardrobe and not easily discarded. Vivian Shelby, the Grand Dame of the department was fond of quoting from one of the sophomore novels - something about sarcasm being the instrument of the weak. Probably so, yet Sloan appreciated a deft turn of the knife.

"We won't," said Barry Rasmussen, the blond, kinky-haired, thick-necked boy who always made him think Oktoberfest and drunken sods

4

in German beer gardens. He sat in the front and fancied himself a comedian. The star of the soccer team, he boasted of having "educated feet." Sloan had once suggested his feet had promise, but the rest of him was hopeless. The self-esteem crowd would have pilloried him for that one too.

"Do you want me to hold your thermos bottle, Mr. Sloan?" volunteered Inez, a thin, cheerful girl with uneven teeth and tumbling, saliva speech.

"Get your homework out." They knew the routine but still the reminder each morning. A dozen or so responded, a handful continued talking, and the remainder sat staring blankly. "C'mon…C'mon…Let's go. We're wasting time."

"Okay! God, give us a chance," a whiny protest from the center of the room which he chose to ignore. Tammy, an All-American name for an All-American pain in the ass. She enjoyed her nasty little jabs when he wasn't looking, knew it irritated him because he could not always be certain it was she. Always the off chance it was Carla or Millie, equally unpleasant creatures, and nothing would please her more than to be falsely accused, the wrath of righteous indignation. A beeline to the counselor.

Sylvia Johnson slipped into the room as he was completing roll. Some mornings a couple of minutes late, others as much as twenty. He had issued tardy slips, written referrals, and attended parent/teacher/counselor conferences. Nothing worked. She should have been suspended long ago, but he knew administration was reluctant to suspend… Anesthesia did not have such students. Instead, all interested parties, "stakeholders" in educationese, a term that always brought to mind ropes and pegs and the folded canvas of a Cub Scout summer or the slaying of vampires, sought obscure reasons for Sylvia's chronic tardiness. She went into counseling, talk even of psychiatric help, at district expense, of course, to uncover some traumatic event from early childhood the lingering effects of which she might still be coping.

"We have to confront that little voice that's controlling you, Sylvia," intoned Louise Randall, the I-P counselor, during a meeting with the afflicted, her mother, and Sloan the week after Winter Break. "You see, Honey, all we have to do is find out what it is and we can beat this together." Mother draped a protective arm around daughter and squeezed; the love was palpable.

"Sylvy, listen to Mrs. Randall. She's on our side," she pronounced, glancing at Sloan, who at the moment was more intent on controlling the gas deep within his bowels and feeling more NRA than PTA, than he was in playing the Sylvy game. "A cork! A cork! My kingdom for a cork!" he might have pleaded but ventured instead, "Maybe she just doesn't want to get up."

All three fixed him with death stares. But his class, first period of the day, was the only one she was habitually late to. Seemed reasonable to him. But he had long concluded that reason was not an integral part of the Anesthesia curriculum.

He had excused himself after the silent staredown and, stepping gingerly down the hall to the restroom, heard Mrs. Johnson complain that it was just that kind of insensitivity that turned kids off from school.

He marked the tardy symbol next to Sylvia's name. He wanted to utter something cutting, damning even, but her defiant expression cautioned otherwise. Besides, on this morning he too was guilty.

Twenty six of thirty four. An average day. After the first two weeks of September, only once had there been a full house. He had noted the date in his gradebook and been tempted to have them introduce themselves. That old demon sarcasm knocking, wanting out again.

"Put your homework on the side of the desk." A quick look and a check next to the name. The entire procedure took about fifteen minutes for short assignments; longer ones he collected. In the meantime they would respond in their journals to the prompt on the board.

Two thirds had completed the work and even then the answers were skimpy at best, but he long ago understood there had to be compromise. He may have been the boss, but he was not the dictator. Too brittle and you broke. He had seen it often enough, young teachers determined to show their mettle and incapable of picking their battles, were eventually overwhelmed, distracted, driven out.

He was amused by the students who tried to pass off a previous assignment or something unrelated in the hope he would be too rushed or too dimwitted to notice. He had little patience with the excuse makers, however, those who wove elaborate tales of why they were unable to complete the work. His favorite was "family problems" or more emphatically" a "family "crisis," which they figured was hard to challenge. If he asked for specifics, then he opened himself up to a charge of prying or not trusting them, which, of course, he did not. Everyone knew Anesthesia enrolled only trustworthy students. Five churches on Wedgewood Boulevard alone. Plus, the mere mention of "family" appealed to the human side, what could be more sacrosanct, but they soon learned Sloan had neither humanity nor family. Then there was always the old reliable: "I didn't understand the question." Joel We-Chi's favorite. Son of a wealthy Taiwanese, he had his own apartment, a new BMW with tinted windows, and a generous allowance. Little incentive for him to extend himself.

Once class was underway, he employed a biting, actually more rip-and-tear humor that, in some perverse way, endeared him to most, perhaps because he did not exempt himself. With Period 1, regular American Lit, though, humor was homeless, transient, too early in the day to really take up residence. A few, Oliver, Blaine, Juliana, the exchange student from Brazil, and occasionally Rachel, showed signs of life, and a hand might go up, but he could never count on even that meager response.

"Okay, now. The big question: Why does Dexter cry at the end of the story." Funereal silence. Sloan himself felt like crying.

"Because he's a wimp." Their blond Pele grinned broadly and looked to take a bow.

"Almost funny, Barry. Now thank your feet…anyone. C'mon. Why does Dexter cry?… I know. I know. With a name like 'Dexter' he should cry. But apart from that."

He turned his back on them and pondered the floor as he strode across the room. The pose invited pensiveness. On evaluation forms it was labeled "modeling." They were to take his lead and concentrate, deliberate, but in fact he was trying to remember if there was anything in the refrigerator for dinner. At the very least the stillness had subdued Rasmussen, who respected peer majority in all things, even silence. A few were smiling stupidly at one another, but most actually did seem to be thinking.

Second semester, sixth week. They were on the Modern Short Story Unit, though for these kids, for whom the Sixties were the Pleistocene and Fitzgerald, Hemingway, and Faulkner, mere cave grunters, "Modern" hardly fit. No, for this bunch last month was a stroll down memory lane. Colonial literature had been a monumental struggle, Jonathan Edwards akin to a week on the rack. *The Crucible* stretched over three weeks. Initially, many were enthusiastic, eager to read a part, already imagining themselves on stage, applause, bows to adoring throngs, Hollywood the logical next step. By the end of Act I, most had lost their desire for stardom and what remained was a Byzantine torture of fractured pronunciation, inverted language and pauses that stretched on like a desert landscape. Not surprising really. Even in this comfortable town, at least a third read below grade level.

"Any volunteers? Be brave. Take a chance!" He hated the coaxing, the near begging. "No volunteers? What happened to motherhood, apple pie, the flag...yes, Frank."

"Is it because..." The boy hesitated. Heads turned. Frank seldom volunteered for anything except to play his trumpet in the talent contest, which he never won, or even placed in the top three. Last year, with only five acts, he was beaten out for the last spot by a freshman who played air guitar. Kid had all the right moves... and all fiction, naturally. He was in the right place.

"Yes."

"I mean...she's not the way he remembers her."

"How does he remember her?"

"Like...like...beautiful, glamorous, ..."

"The title?"

"It's like a dream...he doesn't see her that way anymore. The romance...it's gone."

"Good! Yes. 'Winter Dreams.' The dream is gone!"

So too the rancid chicken breasts he remembered tossing. He would be dining out after all. Not "out" exactly, "take out." Now the only question: Burger King or Jack in the Box?

# TWO

Wayne "The Great Dane" Bengstrom motioned to the two chairs. Sloan took the one closer to the door. Given a choice, he preferred nearer the exit, than not, the type that inhabited the fringes of crowded rooms – a true wallflower.

He often thought he had missed his calling: border guard, light-house keeper, or one of those people who spent their days peering through binoculars from a remote tower deep in the forest searching for fires. Not a hermit exactly, more detached than estranged.

"I'll be with you in a moment, Ian…learned a long time ago how important it was to write things down."

The principal was scratching furiously on a "Things To Do" pad. A violent, spasmodic script that Sloan doubted he could even read right side up; still, he struggled discreetly from across the desk, half expecting to see "Screw Sloan" or "Fuck Sloan Over" somewhere near the top, but all he could determine was that Bengstrom was on the fifth item. "Improve Handwriting" should have been at the head of his list.

Sloan scanned the décor, noting the flag and the framed verse tribute from the student government at Bengstrom's last school. A NASA logo displayed prominently above a 12x16 glossy of the doomed Challenger crew. To the right, photos of the last three varsity football teams and

11

beneath in six inch red and blue, the school colors, A WINNER NEVER QUITS, A QUITTER NEVER WINS. Combined league record 6-20. Colors should have been black and blue. And from the wall opposite in smaller text, Thoreau offered guidance from Walden: "Simplicity, simplicity, simplicity." Henry David had them pegged. No end of simpletons in Anesthesia.

Bengstrom concluded with a dramatic exclamation point, took a deep breath – he was taking in more oxygen these days – and settled back in the vinyl swivel chair.

A great slab of a figure, well over six feet, pants forever slipping, shirts askew under ill fitting jackets, he played the ebullient, down home type to the max, reveling in a kind of cultured folksiness. Sloan could see him in one of those long, white butcher aprons expounding on prime cuts to a parade of housewives or in overalls clutching a large wrench, his thick shanks protruding o from under a sink.

But for many what initially was a charming dishevelment given, his robust persona, had become tedious, embarrassing even. Drawing to the end of the first semester in the last year of his contract and rumor had it not yet having been offered an extension by the Board, he faced an uncertain future.

A former English teacher himself and an unabashed devotee of the Bard, Bengstrom had a quote for all occasions. Hamlet's "To be, or not to be" was inscribed on his memo pads, though Sloan decided, given the man's current situation, "Out, out, brief candle!" might be more fitting.

The perennial staff walk-on in school productions, he trod the boards as one fairly steeped in greasepaint. On Back-to-School Night he concluded the evening's program with a stirring recitation of Kipling's "If" – ever the teacher, "The Great Dane "was especially fond of a moral lesson – to much chagrin and confusion, the former from the feminists in the crowd, the latter those thinking Kiplinger and expecting financial insights.

No matter, "The Great Dane" relished the contact, the social mix: fundraisers, sporting events, plays, especially the spring musical – the crowd, the chatter, the general bonhomie, such was his element. At Friday night football games he donned a varsity jacket and paced the sidelines, slapping pads as players checked in and out, once knocking over little Jeff Kim, the holder, on his way in for a rare PAT. Against arch rival Trenton he addressed the team in moving tones at halftime, drawing upon the legendary Rockne, the immortal Gipper; the boys hadn't a clue. And with a catch in his throat "The Great Dane "led the charge from under the stands onto the field beneath an autumn moon ripe for victory: final score, Trenton 31, Anesthesia 3.

But he soldiered on, the eternal optimist, one not easily deterred. All hardihood and fellowship, a lumbering pleasantness, like the family dog stretched upon the hearth, like cocoa, oatmeal cookies and a blazing fire. Yet nearing the end of his contract, with three consecutive losing seasons and football "the" sport, even at Anesthesia, though Sloan could not fathom why; ever increasing graffiti; declining test scores; increasing drug activity; and the great unmentionable – supposed racial tension, the joviality occasionally went AWOL.

"You know what got me started?"

The best Ian could offer was raised eyebrows. He did not know, nor did he want to know, yet he knew he was about to know.

"The summer after my freshman year in college, I got a job on a local newspaper. Did everything. Combination gofer, copy boy, cub reporter. You name it, I did it. Believe me, I know what it takes to get a publication out… anyway, there was this one old guy, Cedric, from Kentucky. He was constantly writing notes to himself. Could've been anything. Any detail. Always jotting things down. We're talking Old School here, Ian. He chained smoked Camels. Coughing all the time. We used to joke about Cedric's lunch. Same thing everyday. Turkey… Wild Turkey. But you know, Ian, sharp as a tack. Nothing got by Cedric."

"The Great Dane's" head lolled back, sandy-haired, against the high back swivel chair. He chuckled, eyes closed, still amused, then without warning he shot forward, elbows spread and elevated, palms flat upon the desk.

Christ! Sloan straightened up and looked to Thoreau for counsel. A cabin in the woods; Henry David knew what the hell he was doing.

"His stories were 100% accurate.. all the time. And something you'd appreciate, never missed a deadline."

Sloan nodded. Would he ever. "Deadline" for his staff had various meanings. For Alex in Sports it probably meant waiting for a player to collapse in the end zone. He hadn't had a story in on time all year.

"It's not even Spring Break yet, Ian. Do you think we'll make it to June?" The principal grinned his best grin.

"Somehow, I guess… We always do." Sloan reciprocated with a weak smile. He disliked chumminess.

"So how are we doing, Ian?" said the principal, as though they starting again from the twenty.

"Fine. Everything's going pretty well. No problems."

"Good. Good. And the budding journalists?"

"They're fine. Hard workers." He had already heard from Morgan Vigary, president of the Boosters Club, members were upset over Julie's editorial condemning several of Anesthesia's finest. At the Homecoming basketball game a few of the varsity football squad sitting behind the Trenton bench had taunted the coach and team all evening. Afterwards an altercation, challenges to fight, some pushing and shoving. Hector Blanton, a muscular 215 pound tackle, insulted one very overweight, middle age Trenton parent. Julie told him that Hector and the others had been drinking. Sloan gave her the go ahead and advised her to prepare for the backlash; it wasn't long in coming.

Anesthesia High School was very image conscious, but Julie Fanning, conscience of the *Roar* and its finest writer, cared little for images. She herself was not physically memorable: not pretty, not ugly: neither shy, nor aggressive. But relentless and, in her own quiet way, terribly passionate. He could gauge the intensity by the blue strip of vein beneath her left eye. When she was angry or frustrated, it lightened and broadened, as though actually smearing just below the surface of the pale, transparent skin.

No one worked harder or accomplished more. Her position as editor-in-chief defined her. A decision maker, she listened to suggestions but generally knew what she wanted. Polite, unassuming, ... tenacious. Her writing commanded respect, clear and concise, at times arresting, with those little turns of phrases that could not be taught, that separated real talent from mere competence. Administrators gave her a somber respect, and as publications adviser, Sloan hadn't exactly endeared himself to the District Office. And though her graduation would leave a distinct void on the paper, her departure would make his life easier.

"They do a good job. Struggle to meet deadlines sometimes. The odd disagreement...business as usual."

"I know. I know. Wonderful kids, though." "The Great Dane" removed a folder from the desk drawer and placed it atop the "Things To Do" list. He fingered the bank of slack skin that ran directly down his throat from just beneath the chin. "There is one thing, Ian." He hesitated, a practiced awkwardness, but Sloan wouldn't bite. "Do you think maybe the *Roar's* getting a little negative?"

"I'm not sure I understand."

"Don't get me wrong. A fine publication." Sloan considered making a break for the door, like the old Steve McQueen movie "The Getaway."

"What do you mean 'negative'?"

"Well ...take the piece about the football players. Do you really think that was necessary? I know your kids have to report the news, facts are facts. A disappointing season, no doubt about it. But was the editorial really necessary?"

"That's the editor-in-chief's decision. I thought it was well written."

"I agree! Technically excellent." Bengstrom shifted the folder. "That little gal.... What's her name?"

"Julie Fanning." Who was he kidding? He knew damn well what her name was; she had interviewed him often enough.

"Julie... yes. Good writer. Very good writer...but a little negative for my taste. God knows there's enough negativity in the world. And I'll tell you quite honestly, Ian, her words were hurtful to many in this community and on this campus. Listen to this: 'Apparently Anesthesia's gridiron heroes...' 'gridiron heroes'? Little sarcastic, don't you think?"

"Yes, but..."

"Especially since they had such a difficult season; they had such high hopes..." Sloan could not think why. They were not any good. Forget touchdowns. If by some miracle they moved the ball beyond the fifty-yard line, it was high-fives all around. Rarely did they get to the twenty on kickoff returns and then only if a thick fog rolled in.

"I remember Coach Dickerson telling me in September that he and his staff were confident they would make the playoffs...even a shot at League title." League title? What world was he living in? Sloan could have reminded him the last time they reached the playoffs was 1974 and that in a six-team league in which the top four qualified. Not uncommon to get there with a losing record. As for Dickerson, he was the only coach he'd seen run practices with a clipboard in one hand and a bag Doritos in the other. And staff? Staff was Skipper Thompson and his father Skipper senior who sat up in the bleachers and spent most of his time observing the cheerleaders going through their routines on the asphalt basketball courts behind, except on windy afternoons when he went down to lend support to six-foot four, 150 pound Junior, who wore kaki day in and day out, a purple headband and barked commands in a whiny voice that most of the team ignored. "And when the man in charge tells you, who knows better? You gotta believe, right?"

16

"Anyway, listen to this: 'Apparently Anesthesia's gridiron heroes, unable to defeat opponents on the field, took their show on the road, more precisely, into the gym. Like all bullies they were looking for a sure thing.' There's more of the same. And it's cruel, Ian…those words…the sarcasm…have hurt a lot of people." Another pause, dejection, but like emerging dawn, the inevitable recovery. "We want our kids to be happy, don't we? Sure,…we all do." He leaned toward him and lowered his voice. "Some people were very offended by what she wrote, Ian. Very upset. And just between us," he added, dropping to a near whisper, "the Board was none too pleased." An implied threat? Sloan wasn't sure, but he really didn't give a shit. "Didn't make us look very good either. In fact, you have no way of knowing this unless you were there, but I have been told that Julie had her facts awry."

"Which facts?"

Bengstrom slouched backward, extended his fingers and drew them together in a steeple beneath his chin. Ian sensed the principal had gone further than he had intended, not withstanding the contemplative pose, no doubt taken from a movie one of those British films set in an exclusive boys school, the headmaster having to resolve a weighty issue re., morality, integrity, etc.…stiff upper lip and all that in a richly paneled office, clubby, with sumptuous leather chairs, decanter of sherry on the sideboard.

"What's done is done." The steeple collapsed and "The Great Dane" sought the high ground. "You don't have to mention any of this to the girl, but I was told the man, a Mr. Willis, had been making derogatory remarks to the boys. About the school. The community. The boys themselves. You know the sort of unpleasant stuff…I've met with the young men involved and they have assured me they had not been drinking. No one did anything to Mr. Willis."

That was it then. Anesthesia's finest had given their word, their assurance. Enough said. How quickly they capitulated, parents, counselors, administrators even, when confronted with the old reliable: "Don't you trust me?" or the more damning: "You don't trust me!"

Of course he didn't. Sloan could have written volumes on the dishonest little shits. But…this was Anesthesia.

"Julie was there. She saw Hector push the man twice and call him an obscenity. If you want to talk to her, I can…"

"No need. Won't accomplish anything." He waved his hand as though dismissing the absurd. "It's over. What's done is done….as I said, well written…It's just that there's so damn much negativism around, Ian. We don't need to add to it, do we? Troops have a tough enough job, right? Let's keep our kids filled with the brightness of tomorrow. Anesthesia's such a wonderful place. We're lucky to be working here." And for both of us, how much longer, thought Ian. "A little tighter rein, that's all. There are so many good stories to choose from…Enough said. Let's not dwell on the unpleasant."

Sloan wanted to object, was about to object, but in the end did not object. Objection would be futile. Rightness and wrongness irrelevancies.

They concluded by discussing the supposed reason for the meeting – a second semester observation that had to be completed before Spring Break. As a tenured teacher, he was evaluated every two years, a procedure comprising four meetings, including a pre and post observation conference each semester. They agreed to get together next week and set a date for a class visitation and go over the formal lesson plan, which would state objectives, methodology, criteria for evaluation of students and whatever new hoops the state had set in place.

All part of the grand ball, Bengstrom and he partners. You lead, I follow. Fill out the forms, forms designed under laboratory conditions. No Barry Rasmussen with his educated feet to overturn the vials.

But Sloan knew teaching was not a constant, not entirely controlled, at least not at this level. Not always predictable.: A violent, red hot, shaped one way, then another, constantly recast to accommodate. Forms were static, dead. And yet…he understood the need for accountability.

He had no illusions about himself. Not one of the jolly fellows of the faculty lounge, nor a conference volunteer. Basically a loner, preferring the quiet of his room and the *Times* to the chatter of colleagues at lunch. Rarely did he participate in faculty socials, and even less so since the divorce.

So he would dutifully fill out his card, take his cue and step to the music. And when the melody ended, the appropriate box would be checked off: "Retain."

# THREE

He knew better, especially on a Friday, but like the others, was irrevocably drawn to the narrow slots below the stenciled names. What compelled them to make the pilgrimage at least twice daily – hope, desperation, apprehension? An unexpected windfall: a long lost supplementary check for services rendered: chaperoning a dance, supervising an activity on some forgotten afternoon. Perhaps the grand prize – The Publishers Clearing House, a cool million, then one could really clear out. He had concluded long ago that teachers by nature were dreamers; as kids, the last to give up on Santa Clause.

Or were they simply masochists, the magnetic pull of misery in the form of a call slip. The dreaded request for a conference. Argumentative, challenging parents, usually mothers, with ludicrous appeals for extra credit for their little darlings who couldn't or wouldn't do the regularly assigned work.

No Santa, no gifts, only the inevitable ads and brochures, with testimonials from educators in obscure Nebraska towns, urging one to buy class sets of materials guaranteed to transform your slugs into the brilliant, articulate, achieving types everyone knew they really were. Invitations to attend conferences from which you would emerge, for a mere $399, a dynamic teacher who would change lives, the kind they made movies about. Ominous flyers, too, suggesting your pension and whatever meager funds you had managed to scrape together over the years might very well evaporate without proper management.

Yet there was a common thread – contact with the outside world, the real world. In the end perhaps that was the attraction, even on a Friday afternoon.

The 3x5" slip was taped to the inside of the box, fixed to withstand the most merciful of drafts. The "called" box checked above the name. Only this time he was the parent.

After almost five years he still hadn't adjusted to her new name. He read it several times. Evelyn Sloan was now Evelyn Wallace. Same woman, different Evelyn. "Return Call, re; Teddy." Irritated she had rung him at work, he decided he would wait until he got home.


He pushed the gear into reverse, lurched backward and stalled. Could be important…no, whoever had taken the message had not checked the "Urgent" box. Probably some innocuous request or bit of news.

As he pulled out of the parking lot, a group of students hollered, "Have a nice weekend, Mr. Sloan." He waved unseeing. At a red light he watched three boys trailing after a girl in tight jeans. One sang out, "I want your body." The others laughed too strenuously, and she ignored them. A familiar scene. Some things never changed.

He didn't think about her much anymore and preferred only limited contact. The divorce had been amicable enough. Neither had cheated. Simply a drifting apart, that inexplicable void that developed over time, no particular event, no trigger. One morning he awoke to find she had not simply moved to the other side of the bed, she had left the room altogether. Evelyn maintained they had outgrown each other, but insofar as he could determine, it was she who had done the growing.

He had paid child support, but she remarried, a quite successful Century City tax attorney, Devon Wallace, and his money was no longer needed or wanted. Devon wore expensive suits and designer neckties and drove a Mercedes. He too was divorced, though childless, when they found each other and now they shared a magazine life: vacations in Cancun, Puerto Vallarta, Acapulco. Skiing in Vail. Annual excursions to Europe or Asia. Tennis regularly. And Evelyn, at 43 still attractive, did the workout routine three times a week at an exclusive health club.

He approached the bridge and shifted down into the turn without incident. The late afternoon sun spilled gold across the gorge setting the rear view mirror ablaze. He caught a glimpse of the lines beneath his eyes and the developing tracks high up on his cheekbone. Maybe he should grow a beard.

Divorce was common enough. A Southern California tradition. Almost a third of the staff belonged to the fraternity. But somehow he had never quite gotten used to the arrangement. Not that he still loved her, he didn't. Loyalty, he supposed, sentimentality. The way you stuck with old songs because they had once meant something. His father hadn't even bothered with the formality, just moved out.

He no longer regretted the break…but her body, intimate, exclusive for so many years, now given elsewhere…the two of them diluted to old acquaintances. The former life disassembled, boxed, sealed, put on the shelf

A jogger came plodded along the narrow walkway, halter top, bare midriff and black shorts…a shared flesh for seventeen years…the scar tissue on her left thigh, a childhood accident; he was intrigued by its thickness, its coarseness…the slight rise of her belly…the fine strands at the back of the neck…and now….He reached the end of the bridge and glimpsed the retreating figure in his rear view mirror. Strange, how one could just pack up the intimacies and move on.

He pulled the Rabbit into the carport behind his building, a solid mortar, tile roofed structure built in the thirties. The rent was low, less than the other furnished one bedroom, four units in all above an upholstery shop, since his kitchen and living room fronted the heavy traffic below. And an antiquated street lamp with thick frosted globe stood only a few feet away, directly level with the window. At night the illumination cast a noirish glow, reminding him of all the gritty black and white detective shows when he was a kid.

The kitchen was actually a kitchenette, but the other rooms, a combination living/dining room, and bathroom, were large and airy. The one great luxury was the enormous bathtub, a throwback to another era. High, thick, curved porcelain that beckoned. When he was married, he never took baths. No time and always someone at the door. Now there was time and no one waiting.

He soaked lazily, smoking and reading. He quit when Teddy was born, but started again after the divorce, not that he was ever a heavy smoker – half a pack a day at most. After so many years of voices, silence took getting used to. Anything that helped the transition was appreciated.

His rediscovered vice proved bothersome at school. He had never been a morning smoker but after lunch he craved a cigarette and had taken to sitting in his car the last minutes, puffing away like mad. Or an empty stall in the men's room where he might sit and indulge but listening to someone urinate dampened the enjoyment. The only other alternative was to join the few others who had been shunted off to a corner table in the lounge by the increasingly militant majority. Only a matter of time before they would be banished altogether.

He dropped the book to the floor and closed his eyes. She and Devon despised the habit, wouldn't have an ashtray in the house and always waited for the nonsmoking sections in restaurants. They were just as committed to a healthful diet. No red meat. Chicken and fish only. Evelyn had taken nutrition courses at the local college and culinary classes through UCLA Extension. Her pots of greasy chili a lifetime ago. Another woman. Another time.

He slid lower into the lukewarm water and sighed deeply. Topped with extra sharp cheddar cheese and onions and thick slices of French bread slathered with gobs of butter, firm but not hard, his teeth sinking through the white center and working outward to the chewy crust. A couple of beers. His stomach rumbled in tribute. And she had enjoyed preparing it, sometimes experimenting, a little garlic, a splash of Tabasco some red wine. They usually indulged on a Saturday afternoon, those dwindling twilight hours of fall and winter. So nice to come in around four, tired from chores, a little cold. A hot shower, Evelyn's chili and a lazy evening, cozy and warm together. He was always on the lookout for something comparable and had since learned he was not alone in his quest. An entire subculture of chili aficionados roamed the streets. Sentimentalists, always searching, always tasting, but never quite experiencing that long-ago flavor: a mother's, an aunt's, a grandmother's, a local diner's…an ex-wife's, born-again health freak who disavowed any knowledge of the stuff, as one might deny a sordid relationship or a misspent youth.

He reached for the book, then thought "to hell with it" and closed his eyes.

# FOUR

---

"Jesus!" The knocks, precise, abrupt, demanding, he sat up instantly and shivered. The rapping detonated once more. "Coming! Coming!" Stumbling from the tub, he overturned the pack of Kools into the bathwater "Godamn it!" and wrapped a towel around his waist; no time to look for a robe. Even when he was a little kid he had been self conscious about his body, so thin, so white. Now he was merely pale, colorless, with so much more to cover.

The living room was in shadow, only the muted glow of the street lamp outside the window.

"Who is it?"

"Me, Evelyn." He cracked the door.

"What's wrong?"

"Nothing 'wrong.' I just wanted to talk to you for a few minutes."

"Oh…C'mon in…I'll be right back…I was in the tub." She straddled the thresh-old, unable to commit, as Ian rushed down the hallway. By degrees she entered the room, as though passing through a minefield, each step flirting with extinction.

"Didn't you pay your electric bill?"

"Turn on the lamp by the window." He reappeared in a terrycloth robe, a gift from her and Teddy last Christmas, belted snugly across his chest. Odd, but now he would prefer to stand naked on the street than appear bare-chested before her. "Sorry, must have fallen asleep." Just like him, he thought. She does the disturbing and I do the apologizing.

"It's dangerous to fall asleep in the bathtub." She removed her jacket and draped it over one of the two straight-back chairs at the table in the dining/ living room.

"Yeah, I suppose it is...Want some coffee? Tea?"

"Do you have any herb tea?"

"Just Lipton."

He cleared his books from the low coffee table, composed of something that looked like wood but wasn't, and set down the tray. The entire place was furnished in collectibles: the kind found in driveways. He called it Delirium Décor. Furnished by someone under the influence. But then that was the beauty of a furnished apartment. Nothing mattered. Nothing was yours. Unfettered, one could easily slip away.

"How long have you been here?" She hunched on the edge of the couch, as if reclining meant certain contamination.

"Almost five years." He sat facing her in a creaky wicker chair.

"I thought it was just going to be temporary."

"So did I. But you know how 'temporary' is. Sort of grows on you...anyway, it's comfortable. Suits me." She had visited him only once before, not long after he moved in, before she met Devon, and hadn't thought much of it then either.

"Well, how are you?" She gave him an appraising look, crossed her pant legs and surrendered to the couch. "How have you been?" A blue, filmy material slithered across her thigh, a sensual flowing.

"I'm fine. In fact, I was just thinking about you."

"Really?"

"Actually, your chili." She laughed, showing perfect, white teeth. After her marriage, she decided to get retainers. He had thought it silly at her age but said nothing; besides, her teeth always looked fine to him. Devon was supportive. Said she would be "maximizing" her assets. And now precise alignment. "I suddenly had the urge for a bowl of your chili. Still make it?"

"Oh, God, no! Devon would simply die...Did you get my message?"

"Yes. I was going to call you tonight. It didn't say 'Urgent.'"

"No...not exactly 'urgent.'"

"Is Teddy okay?" He realized this was the first he had mentioned his son, his offspring, his bond with this woman. "Has something happened?" She sat staring at the floor and her shoulders began to shake.

"Tell me about Teddy." He found himself next to her on the couch, his arm around her shoulders. A perfunctory embrace, yet he was afraid of what she would say. Drugs? Cancer? "Tell me about Teddy," he whispered and drew her closer. A rich, creamy scent. He stroked her arm, the flesh soft and warm and for a moment, the briefest of moments, the old desire returned, the longing to hold, to be held, to get lost in her.

At Christmas and Teddy's birthdays, quick kisses on the cheek, nothing more. Embraces then seemed unnatural, counterfeit. Now he comforted her as he did when she was coming full term and would awaken in the night, doubtful, scared, convinced of tragedy. "Is Teddy okay?"

"No...not exactly." She politely withdrew, reached for her handbag, large enough he thought for an entire wardrobe, and retrieved a packet of Kleenex.

She arose and walked over to the window, dabbing one eye, then the other. The pants with the glow from the window behind lengthened her, lending a stature, a regalia that seemed incongruous with the tissue. Her body had remained firm, with still enough curve to interest. They were about the same height, but because she looked taller, she had usually worn flats when they went out. He told her it wasn't necessary but she knew he was self conscious and he loved her for that.

Devon, over six feet, was the ideal complement. The first time Sloan saw them together, side by side, he had to acknowledge they were indeed an attractive couple.

"How can you stand that damn light all the time? Would drive me nuts."

Glossy lipstick, set face, precise hair, darker than its natural auburn; this was not the Evelyn who had worn flats for him.

"You get used to it...what's wrong with Teddy?"

"I'm not sure." She took his place in the wicker chair. "He's changed. He doesn't talk much anymore. Stays in his room all the time." Her lip quivered and she clasped her knees with both hands. "He doesn't want to do anything. No interest in anything. And his grades are slipping." She turned an appealing face. "Teddy's always been a good student, you know that. A's and B's."

"Have you talked to his teachers?"

"Yes. They told me he doesn't do his homework, doesn't study for tests."

"What does Teddy say?"

"Nothing. He won't talk to me. If I ask him questions, he brushes me aside. Just stays in his room."

"What does Devon think?"

"Devon...well, you know. He doesn't have any experience with kids, and he's always so busy, especially now with the tax season coming up...a hectic time...crazy busy... He thinks it's just a phase. A teenage phase."

"Maybe he's right. Do you think ...has Teddy ever used drugs?"

"I don't know. I honestly don't know." She gripped her knees more tightly, and leaned back, her arms locked, tight and straight; then without warning, they buckled, the hands collapsed and she went limp. "I've thought and thought. I keep watching for any signs. I haven't noticed anything but...I'm not even sure what to look for. I just don't know.

Teddy's always been such a happy kid and now he's moody and never smiles…remember when he was little. He was the happiest little guy. Remember?"

"Could it be a girl problem? Does he have a girlfriend?"

"No, I don't think so. He was dating someone last year…a nice girl. He brought her home once. They only went out a few times…then it was over. I don't know what happened. He just stopped seeing her."

"Devon's probably right. Just a phase." Sloan felt no more confident diagnosing his son than the man who had replaced him did. Teddy and he had become more like acquaintances who saw one another infrequently to pass a

few awkward hours. There was never any great joy or sadness in those interludes. He tried to fill the role of divorced father. Tried to be a buddy, especially on the last few visits, now that Teddy was getting older. Wasn't that what was expected? Wasn't that his part? The books. The radio psychologists. Quality time…Christ! The poor souls calling in, seeking answers, seeking solutions…and even this…this conversation, predictable, trite. The emotions banal: the entire scene – ex-wife, ex-husband, joining forces to save their son from contemporary demons – was celluloid, small screen, played out every day at school. No end of help givers.. Everyone a confidante. He was weary of saviors, congrats to love. A fever of understanding.

"I've thought about our situation a lot lately," said Evelyn in a new voice. Composed, reflective, analytic. Academic almost. "The divorce and everything. I really believed that Teddy had adjusted well. It's been nearly…what…six…"

"Five years."

"Right…I wonder if…"

"It's not the divorce. I'm sure," he said firmly. He found her new anxiety distasteful. She hadn't seemed very concerned at the time. Anyway, Teddy wasn't a kid anymore. Seventeen in a few weeks, almost an adult, though he realized that age alone did not bring maturity, not where he taught. Hulking near men with emotions of a child, parents reinforcing the limbo, prolonged childhood only without the innocence.

"I wish I knew. I just wish I knew." She crossed her legs and scrupulously removed a piece of lint. To Sloan on the couch, she in the wicker chair seemed a universe away.

"This is a hell of a time to bring up the effects of the divorce."

"Why are you angry?" Her expression had run the gamut: plaintive, hurt, indignant.

"He's your son too. I thought you'd want to know. I wouldn't have come here if I…"

"You're right. I'm sorry." He wished she would leave so he could crawl back to the tub. "It's been a long week. I'm always worn out on Fridays."

"I guess those kids get to you after awhile, huh?" She emphasized 'kids' in that familiar tone, that tone which suggested teaching was not quite real work. Despite the lip service to the contrary, he had come to believe that most viewed the profession as a kind of game, not exactly a career, more an escape from the competitive real world of pay as you go. No guarantees. No tenure.

"Yeah…yeah, they do."

"I admire your dedication. After all this time you still seem so…"

"Dedicated?"

"Yes…Well, you are! How do you do it?"

"I can't do anything else."

"I don't care what you say. It's really…great, admirable." He wanted to tell her how full of shit she was but it would be pointless.

"I'm thinking of going back to school myself. Devon's all for it. My therapist…Did I tell you?…I'm in therapy."

"No, you never said…"

"Yes! Group therapy. Oh, Ian, it's been so rewarding. Done wonders for me. Dr. Hurst has helped us tap into our potential, our other selves, our private selves. The whole group is wonderfully supportive."

"I thought everything was great with you."

"It is…except the business with Teddy. But, you just don't know what life is all about, holed up in this little place."

"When we were first married, we lived in an apartment not much bigger."

"That was eons ago. We were so young. What did we know. But really, Ian…your world is…so limited. So predictable. I mean, look how long you've been doing the same thing. Let's face it, you haven't made much progress."

"What can I say? Predictable guy…easily satisfied."

"I need to feel alive. You have to make life happen. Untapped potential is like undiscovered wealth." He wondered what lecture she had lifted that from. "Know your possibilities. I've just realized I have an artistic temperament." She was eager, radiant as she explained. "I think that's why I always felt there was something missing before. You know what I'm talking about. Remember…you used to write stories."

"I remember." She and Teddy snuggled under the blanket on the couch on winter Sundays, he at the small table in the corner scribbling in long hand, which frustrated her because she wanted to type for him but his script near illegible.

"Same thing." No, he wanted to tell her, it wasn't the same goddamn thing. He wasn't playing. He had a… and she had been part of it. "Now I know how you felt. Only mine is painting, but I think I'm more intense than you were."

"I didn't know you were interested in art."

"That's just it. You really didn't know me…I didn't really know myself. Don't you see." She pulled herself toward him as if she might offer a token, something inscribed, something endearing. "The climate wasn't conducive to my creativity."

"The only thing you were interested in then was Teddy and…" He was about to say "me," but the pronoun lacked reference now.

"Don't get me wrong, Ian. It's no one's fault. Life's a journey. A journey of discovery…I'm attracted to colors and scenes. I'm very visual…Do you still write?"

"No, not anymore."

"Too bad, you should. Very therapeutic to put your thoughts down. Dr. Hurst has us journaling." She fingered her jade bracelet. She was hung in jade: earrings, necklace. Jade was mystic. "You should start a journal."

"I was going to be a great novelist."

"Of course. But you…we were so young. Both of us so…naïve."

"Do you mind if I smoke?"

"If you have to." She frowned and uncrossed her legs. "It's your place."

He retrieved the floating pack, only three ruined., and lit up in the bathroom to minimize the offense. She had him on the defensive again.

"How's your father doing?" she called, and for the first time in the apartment, he had reason to raise his voice. He took a deep drag. Maybe he should finish it there. No, to hell with her.

"Fine. Holding up okay," he said upon his return. Untrue, of course, but he was not inclined to give a discourse on his father's deteriorating health.

"Does he still live in that awful hotel?"

"Still there." Ian smiled and flipped his ash onto a saucer. Evelyn frowned. "Still gets out to Santa Anita. No more Hollywood Park. He can't stand waiting for the buses and the long ride. With his prostrate, when he has to go, he has to go."

"Isn't it dangerous for him to live alone?"

34

"He likes his independence." He resented the false concern and was tempted to suggest that she and Devon take the old man in. They had plenty of room: four bedrooms, pool, and sauna. A regular resort for him. Teddy wouldn't mind; they got along well and he seldom saw his grandpa anymore. "Anyway, he still has a wicked temper. Isn't a convalescent home in the county that would tolerate him."

"Well, if he's happy…what does Pete say?"

"You know Pete, busy, busy." His brother was the quintessential yuppie, 38 but looked much younger, so the gap between them was more like fifteen years than six. Ian sometimes felt more his father than his brother.

"Never seems to have much time for him, does he?" Britt, Pete's wife, a genuine beauty and, to add insult to injury, of course, younger, was a wound, though cauterized by time and distance, that would not heal.

"Pete's out at the beach. I, on the other hand, am close by."

"That's no excuse. You shouldn't be the one who has to take your father to the doctor all the time. Always be checking on him…" she returned to her jade.

"What are we going to do about Teddy?"

"What do you want me to do?"

"Oh, Ian, I don't know. I wouldn't bother you if I wasn't desperate." She smiled sheepishly. "I guess that didn't come out right."

"It's all right."

"Last week he told me he was quitting the basketball team."

"That's not like Teddy. Did he say why?"

"No. We were talking and I asked him how the team was doing and he said, 'I think I going to quit.'"

"Didn't give a reason?"

"None. He never gives a reason for anything. He just said he wasn't interested in basketball anymore. 'It's boring,' he said. I can't figure it out. I thought you might have some insight. I mean, you know, …you work with kids…you must…"

"Evelyn, I'm not exactly the type students confide in. If you want me to, I'll talk to him, but I think we should be careful we don't blow this out of proportion."

"No, you're right…I'll tell you what, next Saturday we're having some people over for dinner, nothing elaborate, just an informal dinner. I'm doing Southwestern. One of the couples have two girls the oldest Teddy's age, I think. Anyway you could come for dinner and maybe get Teddy alone for awhile. Sound him out."

"Yeah I suppose…been awhile since we had a real conversation… if he takes an interest in this girl…could be a romance, then you'll have something new to worry about."

"I should be so lucky."

# FIVE

The phone rang a few minutes before nine. He had just finished a soft-boiled egg and toast, idly sipping his coffee and reading the paper, a Saturday indulgence that initiated the weekend breaks he so looked forward to. The little pleasures of a quiet life.

The voice, a near whisper laden with appeal, still tinged with the Scottish burr, projected its gray self from the other end, like some fog-bound vessel seeking port. A meal that evening at Everett's, a neighborhood restaurant, family style, the old man's favorite. Without a ride he would have to take the bus. Too far to walk, even for him, a man who had never owned a car. When he hesitated and his father jumped into the void, "My treat, son," Ian, overcome with sadness and guilt, relented. He knew his father would never call Pete, out of the question. Too far away, too busy, a successful man with a lot going on. Would not want to bother him.

"What time?"

The quickest route to the hotel was through Anesthesia and past the high school. He made the trek with mixed feelings: on the one hand he wished to avoid the place on weekends, for to be seen by students, even in his car, made him uncomfortable. They would gawk and giggle, surprised that a teacher actually had a life beyond the classroom, one not determined by bells at fifty-minute intervals.

On the other hand, there was an odd fascination in seeing the school unoccupied, the parking lot and athletic field deserted, as though viewing one's own corpse. Like one of those near-death tabloid pieces he often browsed while waiting in line at the store: "I saw myself from above, so calm, so peaceful – death was reaching out to me, but I wanted to live. I chose to go back. To reenter myself. I chose life!"

Wedgewood Boulevard reflected the subtle conflict gripping the town. Quaint storefronts vying with mini malls. A tanning salon, two video stores, a donut shop, one-hour photo and yogurt store challenged the dignity of the grand Mayfair, a former art deco vaudeville palace with marble foyer and brass railings, long ago transitioned into classic movie theater and designated a state historic landmark; Wedgwood Pharmacy, with its still functioning soda fountain; and Sal's Grotto, its menu, Formica tables, high booths, straw encased Chianti bottles hung from the ceiling, a reminder of the days when meatballs and tomato sauce meant Italian cuisine.

Anesthesia's shaded, tranquil streets of California bungalows, big-porch houses with grand stone chimneys, were frequent locales for studios seeking that bygone America, that lost, tranquil idyll. Fourteen-wheelers with their lights and cords and entourages were not uncommon, for Anesthesia had always been a beacon calling one back, returnees seeking to recreate an idealized past for their sons and daughters. But the enclave was changing.

New zoning had allowed for increased apartment construction, and currently pending before the city council was legislation to lift the ban on high rise development downtown. And where once there had been a scattering of Asians, mostly Japanese, there was now a flood of arrivals from Taiwan, South Korea, and lately Hong Kong, with 1997 looming. These immigrants were not "your huddled masses." They had money, many substantially more than the locals, and though they were the strangers, an undercurrent of suspicion abided in them. Their children were generally better disciplined, more diligent, most obsessed with grades. They participated in school activities and rarely missed a class. Robotic in response, they sought to please, sometimes clumsy in their willingness. Sloan knew where it came from, those attempts to determine what the teacher wanted, almost as though the actual learning was irrelevant. They had been instructed from early on what was important. And at graduation it was mostly they who garnered the awards and the elite college acceptances, in turn fueling a resentment and bitterness in several of the landed Anesthesians.

Not that they were all academic superstars. There was a small group, off-spring of wealthy Chinese, who cared little about grades: their future was secure. They drove BMWs, customized Japanese cars or the family Benz and lived self-indulgent lives, while one or both parents remained in Taipei or Hong Kong to run the family business. Coexisting with this group were the apartment dwellers, poorer Asians, banking on their children to bring home that golden future; Mexican and African American families seeking better schools and, in some cases, foregoing home ownership in poorer areas for a two-bedroom apartment in Anesthesia, many not realizing the formative years had already been squandered, bad habits already ingrained, and the great reversals these parents sought rarely materialized.

In the meantime standardized test scores had begun to decline and Sloan marveled that no seemed to grasp of the effect of these and other variables, for to suggest as much, even in Anesthesia, was incendiary. So committees were formed, computers introduced, methodologies altered, workshops attended, still scores inexorably dipped. And the old established families bemoaned their under-achieving schools, yet clung to the time-honored tradition of "excused absences" for ski trips and other special "family activities." And those teachers who objected were branded inflexible, demanding, unreasonable.

A community of fabrication, weaving their fictitious quilt with Fourth-of-July parades, flag salutes. Tots soccer, and Boy Scouts, while many of its young and finest stumbled home in the wee hours, left campus at lunch only to reconvene in the family room to snort, smoke, or sniff their way through parentless afternoons in the "family room."

Little wonder Anesthesia lent itself so well to the movies, thought Sloan.

He was already on the sidewalk, impatient, ill-tempered.

"Damnits, what kept you? I've been waiting almost an hour." The rebuke began just as soon as Ian pulled up to the curb, the pursed lips shaping the complaint as he approached the car. Ian held the door open and waited for his father to complete the slow, cautious descent. "You're never bloody well on time." He gasped from the effort.

"You haven't been waiting for an hour. It's only a little after six."

"Bugger it, I been standing there since five thirty."

"Why did you come down so early?" But he knew why. Like a child, eager for the outing, if only to Everett's.

"People walking by staring at me." He touched his collar and pulled it close to the scraggly neck, a moody silence the entire drive to the restaurant. When they pulled into the parking lot, his spirits rose.

"Busy tonight…they do a good business, Son."

"Yes."

"You know why? Good food, good service, a fair price…not greedy like the bloody Jews."

Ian sighed. It would be a long evening. He had heard this nonsense since he was a child: the Jews were responsible for every ill that came the old man's way.

"They make the best Swiss steak around," he said when he opened the menu, his tongue moistening his lower lip. The menu was superfluous since he ordered the same dish each time: Swiss steak with mashed potatoes, split pea soup and extra butter for the potatoes.

"See…if you weren't late…" the old man complained whey they learned the kitchen had run out of mashed potatoes. He would have to settle for fries.

When they had finished dinner, the old man satiated, he felt compelled to offer a last reminder, "If you were on time, I could've had mashed potatoes….ah, well Son, you have to make do with what you have."

Ian wanted to tell him what an ungrateful bastard he was. He owed him nothing. He wanted to tell him, even at this late date, that if he had ever cared for his family half as much as his own pleasure, he would not be living in a shabby room with nothing to show for his 74 years. A string of indictments he might have uttered, but as he watched his father, the architect of the disaster that was his life, hunched over his plate, the coffee cup rising slowly, a slight tremble, to the pale mouth, he lost the will.

"Son, can we go for a ride?" A weary, mournful request as he struggled with the seatbelt.

"Put it over your shoulder." Ian reached across, let out some slack, pulled the strap taut and buckled it, settling his father in the way he had once secured Teddy.

"Just a little ride around town. I don't want to go back to that bloody room yet."

"Yeah, sure." He had been afraid of this but had no plans, no commitments, no one waiting. Besides, he was a poor liar; seldom could he pull it off over the phone and never in person, Whenever he made a rare call for a substitute, his voice never rang true to him and he was sure not to Delma at the district office. He sometimes thought that accounted for his limited socializing. He had no patience for gossip, was not interested in the daily lives of others.

He resigned himself and headed for Pasadena. They drove along the edge of San Marino, the old man sated, comfortable, peered through the glass.

"Lovely homes, aren't they?"

"Yeah, they're nice."

"We could have had one. With any luck. Bad breaks, son. If I got to California sooner. Forty eight is too old to start again. But your mother, God rest her soul, wouldn't leave her family. Guttersnipin' Russells. Soon as Petey was born I wanted to come out here…but, her family… she was a weak woman, under their thumb. No bloody future in buggarin' Canada."

Ian Sloan, Junior, let him talk; he'd heard it all before. Once, when he was younger, he might have objected, but not now. Now he simply watched the road and waited for the charade to end. "Your mother said it was her wanted to come out, but it wasn't…ah, well, water under the bridge, huh, Old Boy?"

"'Water under the bridge,'" repeated Ian. That his father, a lazy drunk whose wife had to go herself to the factory to pick up his check, what there was of it, was no longer relevant. Too late truth.

"Remember our little house in Canada, son? You and me practically rebuilt it. Put in our own basement, Remember, Ian, all the bloody trouble we had with that bloody cement truck late and the rain. Bloody hell. Remember how hard it rained, Son?"

"I remember."

"What a bloody mess, Jesus boy-oh-boy… but we got it done, didn't we, Old Boy? We worked good together didn't we, Son?"

"Yes we did."

It had begun to drizzle by the time they got back to the hotel. He unbuckled his father's seatbelt, went around to open the door and watched as the old man shifted his legs to the side and set his feet down on the curb. He placed one hand on the door frame, rose somewhat and sat back breathing deeply. He gathered himself, gripped the door frame again and floundered with his free hand, sensing he would need both for support but uncertain where to put it. Ian hesitated, reluctant to help, nor did the old man ask. He knew it would be uncomfortable to touch him, and when finally he did so, gripping tightly to hold the weight, he was surprised at the smoothness of the palm and it occurred to him that he could not remember holding his father's hand when he was a child.

"Come up for a few minutes, Son."

"I don't think…"

"If you don't have time…"

"Okay…a few minutes."

His mother had told him they should have gotten more, much more for the house, but the visas were about to expire and they had to sell quickly. Afterwards a long train of rentals, their lives, others' rooms. And except for the years with Evelyn in their two-bedroom fixer upper, here he was again, like father, like son, a perennial renter. His father's legacy, thought Ian, as he followed the stooped figure grasping the handrail up to Room 8.

"Sit down, Son." The old man motioned him to the tattered armchair next to the bed, which dominated the room and switched on the 13" black and white Zenith, the dirt and grime on the screen so thick the picture was grainy.

"How 'bout a cup of Dad's coffee?" Again, like all the other requests that evening, he could not decline. The coffee, brewed on the hotplate with water from the tap at the same sink where he shaved and mixed with Carnation canned milk, seemed a fitting conclusion.

He watched his father putter about the messy room, waiting for the coffee to percolate. He navigated, his restricted world in a practiced shuffle: around the bed, over to the closet and back again, absorbed in a range of unseen tasks that only he knew, until the coffee was ready. Ian gave up the armchair for the edge of the unmade bed and they watched a "Kojak" rerun.

When "Trapper John, M.D." came on, the old man took out his teeth and placed them in a jar with baking soda and water and set it next to a western paperback on the small table next to the bed. Midway through the program he fell asleep. Ian stepped carefully to the sink, dumped his coffee and ran water over the grinds. He gently nudged his father.

"I'm going now, Dad."

"Huh? Oh, ah…must have dozed off," he garbled, bleary eyed, through toothless gums.

"Don't get up. I'll lock the door."

"Thanks, Son. We had a good time, didn't we?"

"Yes, we did. Goodnight, Dad."

"Goodnight, Son. And, Ian," raising his hand and leaning on the arm of the chair he added, "rooms" 16, 18, they do some drinking Saturday nights. That's

their bloody radio going. Be careful on your way out. Don't pay them no mind."

"Okay, I won't."

"The Polack…He's got a gun. He was showing the bloody thing around…Got it in for Pepe, the Mexican boy. I don't know why."

"Okay, Dad. Goodnight."

"Call me sometime. Gets kind of lonely in this bloody place. If you remember…If you can."

"All right. I will."

No Pepe. No Polack. He passed an open door but kept his eyes on his ever growing, distorted image in the cracked mirror at the end of the hall.

# SIX

"Just because it's old, doesn't mean it's good," protested Charity Murphy after he had berated them for not having finished the novel. His lecture on the role of setting in character development set aside for another day or discarded completely. Laziness, indifference. He wanted to tell them what fools they were; with little education they would become as trapped in their environment as Ethan was in his. Unfair, he knew, to those few who had actually done the reading, but he was not in the mood for fairness Not so long ago, those who failed to complete an assignment were in the minority; now, except for the Honors classes, they were often the majority, a student body increasingly dividing itself into the "haves" and the "have nots," the few who would prosper with any curriculum, any teacher, any methodology, and the many who would continue in their inadequacy, regardless of subject, teacher, or approach. And their numbers would only increase. A bleak prognosis thought Sloan.

"Age alone does not determine quality. Almost all novels published a hundred years ago are no longer in print."

"I don't care. It's boring." She slouched defiantly in her "Sluts on Fire" t-shirt, the itinerary running down her spine: New Haven – Aug. 23, 1987; Boston – Sept. 8, 1987; Syracuse – Oct. 3, 1987, and so on down to San Francisco on December something descending into her jeans. He imagined "Los" on one buttock "Angeles" on the other. She had probably committed the dates to memory, but could not, over two weeks, read a short novel, one of the fine creations of her culture.

"How would you know it's boring if you haven't read it?"

"I read some of it."

"Actually, there is great passion in the story. If you had read far enough, you might have seen that." He was making a foolish blunder allowing himself to be drawn into the exchange. Inexcusable. Even rookies quickly understood. Everything to lose and nothing to gain. Brought down by adolescent indignation, nothing more. Not logic, not ideals. Only pure, unadulterated bitchiness.

"I guess you have to be old to like that kind of passion." Monica Wells in her "Pain Terrain" shirt offered a toothy grin. A few others smirked. Charity had won.

They read silently for the remainder of the period. While they read, or pretended to do so, Sloan drew an X through Period 4 in his notebook and was reminded of the framed scroll on the door of VP Stan Dugan's office: "Learning is the road to discovery, the teacher as guide lighting the way for those who follow." Dugan had abandoned the trail after two years and moved into Administration.

Sloan perused his fellow travelers: David Jackson, sleeping in the corner; Hyun Kim, discreetly picking his nose; Jasper Lopez, twirling his pencil, staring off into space; Burton Rudemenkin, fingering his Walkman. They had all made U turns. But there was Gloria Liu, newly arrived from ESL, mouthing the words slowly as her finger edged across the page.

Perhaps he was wrong. Maybe it was dull; maybe he expected too much. He opened the book at random…the description of the farmhouse kitchen. A few sentences and he could see the starkness, feel the chill…the confinement, the hopelessness…the oppression became his.

On another page he saw the winter sky at night, the brittle stars, and still later their desperate longing and Mattie's warm breath in the frigid moonlight on the hill above the town. That moment, that prelude to misery. No, he was not wrong.

The bell, the rush to the door.

"Yes, Richard?" The boy had approached with an air of familiarity, of unwarranted confidence that irked Sloan. Nothing tentative about Richard Lyon "Mr. Sloan, what grade am I getting?" The self impor-tance, the classic assumption that he should have the boy's grade on the tip of his tongue simply because…because he was Richard Lyon.

"I don't have any grades tallied. Not until the end of the quarter."

"I mean, you know, approximately."

"Well, let's see." He opened the gradebook, Lyon, Richard: "You took a C- on the last test and…"

"I know. I thought I did good. I don't understand. I studied for that test, too."

"Don't you study for all the tests?"

"Yeah…but…"

"I'd say you're about a C." He looked again. "Between a C and a C+." He added the plus for motivation.

"I can't get anything less than a B," the boy said matter-of-factly. "If I get a C in any of my classes, I won't get into a good college." Was this a deli? Ham on rye, hold the mayo. I don't eat mayo…I don't take Cs.

"You better get to work then. There's still enough time to bring up your grade. But you can't get less than a B in the remaining work.

"I'm really trying hard. I really studied hard for the last test."

"How long did you study?"

"I don't know…couple of hours."

"Wasn't enough then, was it? Maybe you should have studied four or five hours."

"Your tests are too hard." His eyes narrowed. Gone the comfortable, self-assured boy-next-door. "Your tests are harder than the other teachers."

Sloan recognized the ploy immediately: Suggest he didn't measure up, was inferior to his colleagues. And it worked on some, the younger teachers especially and those few regardless of how many years in the classroom still plagued by self doubt. Some of these kids had radar; didn't take the little shits long to pick up on the insecurity.

"If you're not prepared, they are." Gloria Liu, who could barely speak English two years ago, had the third highest grade on the test. He knew she was up half the night poring over the text.

"I studied hard!"

"Look, if you want to discuss this any further, come by after Period 7." He made for the door, Lyon at his heels.

"Oh…I'm supposed to tell all my teachers…I'll be absent the first week after Spring Break. My mom's taking me back East to look at colleges."

"You can't afford to miss that much time if you expect to improve your grade."

"I can't help it. College is an important decision. It's my future… do you know anything about Colgate?"

"Not really. Sort of a second level Ivy League school, I think.."

"Ivy League!"

"You need very good grades and SAT scores to get in."

"That's what I mean. I can't get any Cs," he reminded him before sauntering away and Sloan wanted to call out to him that the only Colgate he would ever experience was in the drugstore. He watched Anesthesia's own stroll across the grass, the backpack, slung over one shoulder, more ornamental than functional. A basketball star on a mediocre varsity at a small high school in a lower tier league. If he was lucky, he might make a community college team, where he would probably end up.

How did it come to this? He could never quite figure it out. Who nurtured the unreality? The illusion. Parents? Counselors? Teachers? Coaches? Maybe all of them, a conspiracy in the name of "self esteem." They all simply wanted "our kids" to be happy. Then by the end of March senior year, the thin envelopes, the brief rejections, like a hammer blow, a sudden jolt that would leave many dazed for weeks. By graduation most would have accepted this first real brush with truth, inflexible, concrete, they had no choice. Until then, they need not. Until then they could remain the stars, the beauties, the prospects in their enchanting fantasies.

"Mr. Sloan! Mr. Sloan!"

"She's not here, Gordon. She's already left." At 5'5" and just over a hundred pounds, draped in black: shoes, pants, Metallica t-shirt, black hair, and black binoculars dangling on a sunken chest, he looked more like one of the large crows that haunted the campus, than the high strung, smitten Gothic sophomore he was.

"Are you sure? Are you sure, Mr. Sloan?"

"Yes, Gordon. I'm sure."

"Sometimes teachers think someone's there and they're not…they get confused when they're taking roll…I mean, they mistake people."

"Gordon!" He hadn't meant to raise his voice, but the clock was ticking. Yet he knew the kid was right; teachers did make mistakes with attendance. "Melissa was here. She left a few minutes ago, with Paula and Jean. Check the quad."

"I just came from there. I didn't see her. She's not…"

"Gordon!"

"Yes, Mr. Sloan."

"Go to lunch."

Twelve precious minutes had slipped away by the time he reached the faculty cafeteria. Normally he brought his own lunch, but since he had gotten up late, he would have to settle for a packaged sandwich, one of those cellophane wonders, probably corn beef, which would wreak havoc on his upper intestine around 6th Period. And depending on Beatrice, he would have, give or take a few, only twenty minutes to eat, glance at the sports section, and possibly use the restroom.

Beatrice appeared old enough to have already been long established in Food Service at the advent of Social Security, yet apparently had still not reached full benefit status. A withered figure with beige accordion face, its folds gathered in a perennial apprehension that dispersed whenever she spoke. Having endured a litany of complaints about food and prices over the years, she had become the very definition of torment. Anything could set her off. A scowl at the chef's salad she might take to heart and in absolute misery either overcharge or undercharge, adding further to the agony. In that already mottled brain a nickel might become a quarter, Washingtons, Lincolns, and what began in innocence would end in guilt. Once she had given Ian $4.50 in change for a dollar which he made the mistake of pointing out and for days afterward she would not acknowledge him, his transactions processed through whoever was before or after him in line. And on those occasions when the anxiety had grown intolerable, she would abandon the counter altogether, staggering back through the swinging doors into the kitchen where she breathed deeply, a breath constricted by a lifetime of Camels. The coughing would start and everyone waited dutifully for the war in her lungs to subside, whereupon in due course, she would emerge, bent and shaking, but unvanquished, to resume her duties. She was the most dependable of the kitchen staff. Never missed a day, much to the chagrin of her clientele.

"Hand me a Diet Pepsi, will you Ian?" Roth, also late, was quieter than usual, though the stark menu tended to have that effect: cold sandwiches; wrapped, micro salads of dying lettuce and soggy tomato slices; steam-heated burritos. Occasionally spaghetti, noodles only, no meatballs, in a tomato sauce, just a reminder the stoves were still operational.

Yet they could pretend, and wishes did sometimes come true. Last February, a rainy Wednesday the staff spoke of in reverential tones, a mythic time, one of those occasions from which legends spring. On that afternoon, inexplicable really, for there had been colder, rainier days, soup. Real, homemade, hot soup, thick, creamy chicken with actual morsels of the bird. The unlikely warming scent greeting them as they arrived, damp and glum. Manna from the gods, at the ungodly price of $2 for a small Styrofoam cup. But they gladly paid. A marvelous day for Beatrice; she was fairly radiant, a delight to witness as she spooned up the heady mixture and handled all business in a timely, accurate fashion, addressing everyone by his proper name. Alas only a teaser, one day only, in retrospect, a sadistic reminder of what might have been.

"Poor thing," whispered Sharon Mallory, choir director, "she should be put out to pasture."

"Reaganomics," said Sloan from behind his hand. "No more pastures."

"You got that right," added Roth.

"Yes. Yes, Mr. Slomes. Yes. Yes." The breathing was uneven, strained, as she gripped the counter. He shouldn't have covered his mouth. "Can I…Can I…help you? I don't want to rush you. But, but…I do my best, you know…I do my best." Fortunately he had the exact amount and made a hasty retreat.

"Ian, got a minute?" Roth was slouching behind sipping his Pepsi. "I need to talk to you about something."

"Sure." So much for the Sports page, probably the restroom as well.

Roth took Rasmussen's seat and unwrapped an Anesthesia burrito. "Good stuff. Imported all the way from Pico Rivera. From our family to yours."

"Good shit," agreed Sloan as he pulled the cellophane from a tuna salad sandwich; Beatrice's selection, not his. He had specifically said "corned beef," very slowly. Beef? Tuna? He must have missed the connection. One consolation – he was less likely to be stricken later.

"Look at this, man. $1.50 for a goddamn bean burrito. That's outrageous. Our own school ripping us off." He bit into the grayish dough and slurped up the beans and sauce.

Roth was their resident lefty. No one would ever take him for an ex marine. Slight, scruffy, anemic, of average height and terrible posture. Tinted glasses above a dry, wayward beard of the same hue as the unkempt cotton candy that swirled around encroaching baldness. About forty, Sloan figured, but he looked older.

Raised on corn-belt patriotism in a small Ohio town. Humid, watermelon summers of muted front-porch conversations at dusk and bitter, slaty, prairie winters, an endless shutting down, the hoped for spring somewhere beyond the horizon. He had enlisted right out of high school, served a tour in Vietnam and returned a committed, anti-war activist. And somehow along the way amidst, the speeches and demonstrations, from Chicago to San Francisco, picked up a college degree. He lost count of the schools. A course here, a course there, eventually all coming together in a B.A., with credits to spare.

Roth taught American History and taught it well. Though he had grown somewhat more moderate, he continued an undeclared war against administration, and since he had known real war, remained unfazed. None of the skirmishes ever amounted to much. His most recent, Dugan's objection to *Mother Jones*, which he had noticed on Roth's desk when he dropped by for an unannounced observation.

Dugan insisted the magazine was inappropriate in his classroom. Perhaps college, though he had his doubts, where they entertained a variety of opinions, no matter how extreme. Leafing uninvited through the pages he was particularly offended by a cartoon of the President and strongly suggested Roth stick with *Time* and *Newsweek*, both of which the library subscribed to. And more than one of Anesthesia's matrons had complained of his lectures, too far left for their right thinking offspring. Roth ignored them but was obligated to sit through one of Bengstrom's Rotarian spiels about "the heavy weight of responsibility" they all shared.

He knew the score. The "offended" were usually obnoxious little jerks who were not doing well and this was payback. He could care less. He was well aware the Dugan and Bengstrom would love nothing better than to catch him screwing up. But he knew also he was a good teacher. And the students knew it too, as did Dugan, though loathe to admit it. Roth made them work, but he also made them think. He was well read and Sloan generally agreed with his political views. And since they shared many of the same students they communicated regularly.

"See where that putz Reagan fell asleep during the arms conference? It was on CNN. Old Ronny catching Zs and they're going on without him. Jesus, Commander-in-Chief, asleep at the switch…anyway, Ian, I wanted to ask you about the *Roar's* letter policy.

"What about it?"

"You take letters from teachers, don't you? I can't remember ever seeing any."

"Sure, faculty can submit if they want. Haven't had any for quite a while…I think Sammy's a few years ago. Remember, when he retired? His farewell letter."

"Oh, yeah, old Senile Sammy. Everybody but Sammy knew his kids cheated like hell. Biology with Sammy was an easy A. You'd think he would have wised up…eventually. He had more A's than anyone,,, easy grader. But he never did. Loveable guy. I guess no one had the heart to tell him what was going on. Sammy had more TA's than the rest of his department put together. Christ, I bet Leonard Tupper made a fortune selling his tests. Remember Leonard? Nobody'd write the little bastard a recommendation.

"Wasn't his mother head of PTA or something?"

"Oh, yeah…poor, freakin' Sammy. He thought they were all angels. Remember how emotional he got at the assembly when they gave him the gold pin? Man, 35 years. Retired two weeks and bam! Freakin' diesel truck…Blew his ass to bits. You know what's weird?"

"What?"

"He told me once that he was afraid to drive on the freeway… stayed in the slow lane."

"You're really cheering me up."

"All right, back to the letter…I'm really pissed about something and I was thinking of writing a letter…you know, sort of an open letter to the school community."

"About what?"

"Mrs. Sobel and her Holocaust video. Bengstrom wants all classes to see it again this year. They study the Holocaust in World History. Plus we touch on it in American History and the kids read *Anne Frank* in Freshman English. But it's her pet project, ever since her trip to Israel. I thought it was just a one-time thing last year, but she wants it mandatory viewing for all history classes every year. I shouldn't have to give up a couple of periods for something they've already seen. We lose too much time as it is with all the bullshit going on around here. I have plenty of material to cover."

"What does your department say?"

"They agree, but you know…they all go along to get along. I suggested at our last meeting we prepare a statement, sign our names and give it to Bengstrom. But you know Suds. She likes being Chair. She's a kiss ass. Doesn't want to antagonize Bengstrom. And you can't expect anything from Dugan. He's a rubber stamp. Only concerned about one thing – Stan Dugan."

"The Administration Code – 'Honor Thyself.'"

"You got that right."

"So what's the letter going to say?"

"I don't know yet. Something about outside influence on the curriculum. Meddling. That sort of thing. You know damn well she told Bengstrom what she wanted to do and he rolled over. She's a Board member; what's he gonna do? He's worried about getting his contract renewed. Remember the code:"

"Honor thyself" they said in tandem.

"But you know, Tom, some might accuse you of being anti-Semitic. You don't want to have to deal with that."

"For Christ's sake…I'm half Jewish!" he exclaimed with the remains of the burrito.

"I'm just telling you how some people might react."

"Will it make trouble for you?" He removed the glasses and rubbed pale blue eyes encased in startlingly white sockets, an albino contrast to the dark lenses.

"No. No. I'm already on Bengstrom's shit list. Don't worry."

"What happened?"

"Julie's editorial on the football players. He's pissed."

"Did he call you in?"

"Oh yeah, but he knows she's right."

"Of course she's right…arrogant jerks. Fine piece of writing, Man." He offered a shaggy grin. "Hell of a writer. She's a killer, goes right for the jugular. I loved having her in class. Really bright. No bullshit about her. Idealistic, but tough. She's going to be something."

"She'll be the one you submit the letter to."

"Look, Ian…seriously, I don't want to cause you any grief."

"Don't worry about it. Go ahead and write the letter. We don't edit them so watch your grammar."

"All right. I'll start on it tonight. When do you need it by?"

"Deadline for next issue is Thursday the twentieth. Just put it in my box and I'll pass it along to Julie."

"Sounds good…you know, maybe that's what I'll do if I leave this place. Write a letter to the newspaper, parting words. Dugan, Bengstrom, few others. Tell them what sorry motherfuckers they are."

"I'd sign on to that."

Sloan checked the clock and deducted seventy six minutes. The repair request had been submitted last November. His students called it "Sloan Time." Different zone altogether.

Three minutes. Not even time for a piss.

# SEVEN

He awakened to rain. Through the open living room window, down the hall and across the threshold of his bedroom, a sibilant refrain punctuated by the intermittent swish of tires, churning, spitting upward from the pavement below.

He rolled onto his stomach, his head dangling over the side of the mattress and stared at the carpet, a diamond pattern of green on copper. No inspiration to move there. Why couldn't he sleep late like other people? He awoke early every day, even weekends. The alarm in his head now. A sign you were getting old. Lying on the stomach was supposed to be unhealthful he remembered and immediately rolled back, while recognizing the absurdity: he smoked, got little exercise, and had a spotty diet at best. Well, at least they would find him right side up.

Another Saturday with Saturday's agenda: breakfast, a little cleaning, grocery shopping, reading, perhaps some schoolwork. No, not quite the same. Evelyn's dinner. The business with Teddy.

"Goddamn it, Jerry." Sloan flipped onto his stomach and pressed the pillow across the back of his head. The Harley thundered three, four times before roaring out of the parking lot and down the alley. Why not a Yamaha, Kawasaki? Quicker acceleration, hell of a lot quieter. Jerry

Nagoya had the apartment across from his and worked in an auto parts store, so Saturday was just another day.

Could at least show some godamn loyalty. What the hell ever happened to Asian pride? "Dumb shit!"

The living room was chilly, the carpet beneath the window damp to his bare feet. He hit the top of the frame twice with his elbow and it popped loose and dropped shut. He peered at the streetlamp, the dripping globe directly across from his window. From his vantage point he could see clearly the intricate iron work at the top of the column. The effort seemed wasted. People did not look up at streetlights. When he was young, rain was dreamy, romantic, that indulgent melancholy when you were alone and yours was the only world, the rain of youth. The rain of middle age was simply bleak.

He shaved and retrieved the newspaper at the foot of the stairs beneath the mailboxes, and over coffee, toast, and eggs, read the sports section and contemplated the day ahead. He considered calling Evelyn with some excuse; his presence or lack of it, would have no great effect. But there was the matter of Teddy. He knew she was counting on him. Her worries, like her interests, were excessive and passing. Still, she had made the effort to come by. And there was Teddy.

Sloan had long felt disconnected from his boy. Theirs was a peripheral contact amidst another life – a Devon and Evelyn sphere, one alien to his own, their meetings mechanical, remote. And what could he say that Teddy hadn't already heard? What did she expect from him? Sure he was concerned, but not really worried, at least not enough to go running panic-stricken to his son, begging to be let in, begging him not to throw away his future.

After working with teenagers for so many years, he felt he knew them. If you took everything they said literally, everything they did at face value, then all was lost. Hyperbole was their life's blood. Whatever they said, divide by three. There were exceptions, of course, there always were. That was the problem.

He understood for most parents, adolescence was a maze, like the convoluted rows of shrubbery he had once seen on a travel show featuring British estates with extensive, complex rows of shrubbery leading guests from one turn to another until quite unexpectedly they stumbled out into the open.

And for the frantic, over-protective ones, the ones who lay down at night in perpetual anxiety and arose each morning in apprehension, other kids were sex-crazed, drugged out, dishonest cretins just waiting to prey upon their innocent little darlings. Next to their view, nihilism was the power of positive thinking. As for himself, it wasn't selfishness that kept him from Teddy. And he couldn't plead lack of time, too consumed by the lifestyle and work that usually explained the absent father. God knows he had enough experience with that at school. He loved Teddy, but if he were perfectly honest with himself, he would acknowledge that the love was more instinctive than conscious. He would do his duty, though, and in a private moment would try to get some understanding of what was troubling the boy.

After breakfast came the cleaning, which he did not especially like or dislike, just another part of the routine. When he did housework, he dug out the old LP's he had carried with him through the years, packed, unpacked, repacked. Probably the only person in LA who still owned vinyl and a machine to play it on. His old favorites: Sam Cooke, Dinah Washington, Roy Orbison, Brooke Benton, a few others. He finished the dishes to "September in the Rain," Dinah's plaintive sound returning him once again to the sweet melancholy of youth.

Sloan roamed the aisles with the vague idea he should eat better, healthier, though in the end, taste would win out. Gradually, with many stops and starts, he accumulated a week's provisions. He operated from memory, however, a memory he knew was fallible when, usually by Thursday, he had run out of something. Others with their lists and meticulous checking as they scanned the shelves brought a surge of guilt, compounded when he sometimes found a discarded paper in the bottom of his cart, items neatly grouped and ticked off, the occasional notation: "for Annie" or "only on sale." Their thoroughness underscored his deficiency yet simultaneously providing a glimpse into another life. And he might speculate for a moment about the shopper, whom he always assumed was a woman. And who was Annie? Daughter? Sister? Friend? Were they hard pressed, or merely thrifty. The latter he decided. The consummate mother, ever vigilant, ever protective of the family welfare. For all he knew, his mystery shopper might well be male, middle age. An unemployed house painter trying to make ends meet or if female, an elderly lesbian on a fixed income.

He stacked his usual load on the conveyor belt: ground beef, chicken, pork chops, nothing exotic. Some frozen foods, a few fresh vegetables, half of which would probably spoil before he could eat them. And his spiritual indulgences: a can of garbanzo beans, a tin of salmon. He liked the beans but it was the label that impelled him, a golden harvest on a shiny, black band. The salmon a holdover from childhood, when the fish was a luxury and eaten only on Fridays.

"Hi, how are we today?"

"Fine," said Ian. He replaced the Readers Digest in the rack. Once again a B on the vocabulary quiz. He had yet to crack the A zone. If his students only knew.

"Ginny," she chewed and called to the checker at the next register, "have you seen the new 'Indiana Jones'?"

"Not yet."

"Me neither. Ben wants to see it. I like Sean Connery."

"So do I."

"He's old, but kind of sexy." She smiled at him as she rang up the next item and he caught a glimpse of the purple wedged behind the back teeth. Was it his imagination? Was she… "And they say there isn't a lot of violence; it's kind of fun violence, you know what I mean… Oh, guess what?""

"What?"

"I got Ben a rabbit. He just loves it."

"You did?"

"Yeah, last week. You should see it. He's a cutie. Brown and white."

"Manager okay with it?"

"He doesn't know; I haven't said anything." She looked at Sloan, "We're not supposed to have pets." He smiled weakly. He hated the chattiness and usually avoided her check stand. Her hair long and dirty blond appeared coarse, like straw, not the tresses a man would bury his face in unless he wanted to clean his pores. She was busty, a block figure, solid. Just above the right breast a pin that read: "Grace Wagner – Bronze Circle – Five Years Service." She had big hands, no doubt big legs. In her apron uniform a cross between teen and matron, Aunt Bee the Vixen.

"$46.91, Mr. Sloan." He gave her a check and waited as she completed the transaction.

"Kind of stupid to check I.D. I know who you are… but rules are rules… I also know how old you are," she added with a wink. She handed him the receipt and the driver's license allowing her fingers to touch his palm. "How's school?" He looked up quickly, startled almost, as though a gun had been discharged. She was beaming. "How are the little monsters?"

"Fine. They're fine." Then he remembered once in an unguarded moment, when he had first moved into the neighborhood, he had gotten caught up in conversation. She had told him he looked just like her old high school English teacher and wasn't it weird, cosmic almost, that he taught English too. He had agreed it was indeed and made a point to avoid her in the future.

"You keep after them. Teachers are so important."

He put away the groceries, grabbed a beer and flopped down on the couch. The bathroom needed cleaning but it was still raining and he had enough of water. North Carolina was playing Iowa State. Carolina was leading but he really couldn't get interested. He picked up a transcendental essay from Period 5, the stack a painful reminder of what lay ahead. Wilhelm Stephens. A good student, bright, responsible, but arrogant. Had to be the name. Delusions of grandeur? Who would burden a kid with a tag like "Wilhelm"?

Iowa State called a timeout and the players gathered around their coach who was probably making twenty times what Ian earned. Sloan tossed the paper back on the coffee table. Student athletes? What a joke.

He slid down the couch and closed his eyes. Play had resumed but he was already drifting. He thought of his father upstairs in his room. The old man liked sports, but not basketball. Boxing and soccer... real football ...international sports, baseball American, a distant third. He had instructed Ian in the manly art, how to use the jab to set up your opponent. How to anticipate and counterpunch.

When he was in a good mood, when he wasn't drinking, evenings could be pleasant. They might push back the furniture and play marbles on the hardwood floor, his mother watching, listening to the radio and sewing, a respite from the tension, the violent language...the violence itself. Now there was no one to frighten, no one to bully...only death waiting, waiting to...

He was transfixed by the gun at the end of the Polack's dangling arm pointed at the floor. A two-barreled, sawed off shotgun. A Mexican kid stood beside him at the end of the hall, both staring at him as he

64

approached. The Mexican dropped his eyes and blessed himself as Ian, struggling with his burden, drew near. He paused at the top of the stairs to strengthen his grip. A slow, precise maneuvering as he anticipated the stair with the torn, rubber matting. He found it and eased to the side, stopped and leaned against the wall, the load heavier than he would have imagined.

He stepped into the lobby, the body in his arms, as though it were a ceremonial offering. The lobby window, with the word HOTEL in black letters, an elegant script trimmed in gold, fronted a busy street, people hurrying by, eyes straight ahead. A faded maroon and blue carpet, and along the walls rubber plants in their indomitable, waxy greenness, hulking in tarnished urns. Elderly men sat smoking or reading newspapers in high backed, worn chairs. A few, engaged in low conversations, stopped talking and stared when they saw the lifeless cargo. He wanted to say, "my father" but the words would not come. He wanted to tell them…to explain…

He jerked awake in a cold sweat, his mouth dry. In the bathroom he rubbed his face with the cold washcloth and drank two glasses of water, one after the other. He sat on the edge of tub and shivered. So vivid, so real. He could still feel the give of the stairs under his feet, still see the denizens reading, chatting…waiting their turn. Upstairs everything had been the same, but his father's hotel had no lobby, only a narrow entry way. Not his father's hotel, but so vivid he felt he should recognize it but he didn't. A big city hotel, once grand, but gone to seed. But definitely downtown, not the suburbs. He had always liked downtowns, the immediacy of store-fronts and office building doors, the nooks and crannies, the narrow passageways where sunlight divided and subdivided in hard chasms.

He recalled a trip to Detroit when he was little, five or six. His mother's side of the family, an uncle or cousin; he couldn't remember.

They never did meet up with the man. They had to pass through skid row, a few dreary blocks in the central city, and he remembered being both distressed and fascinated by the derelicts, the broken lives sprawled in ragged costume along the sidewalks. Some called to him, laughing derisively. One in bearded, grimy face and matted hair, swathed in garments of multi shaded filth, grabbed at his shoe, flipping the separated sole up and down and pointing at Ian, the blistered, purple lips spread wide in gap toothed grin. He had pressed his mother's hand, but remained hypnotized by the mocking figure.

He was washing his face a second time when he remembered.

# EIGHT

The rain had stopped and in the night a newness, the stretch of free-way glazed before his headlights as he approached the 134, the foothills to his left immediate and dark, to his right the L.A. skyline off in the distance.

There was little traffic, but like most dreading an encounter, he took his time, dropping to fifty in the slow lane. He rolled down the window and the cold air whipped his face. Blinking rapidly he took deep breaths inhaling the scent of the shrubs that grew up to the edge of the guard rail. On the edge of Pasadena, he curved onto the 305 and saw JPL to the right, settled, dignified, consequential, a beacon.

In the scientific realm, JPL was Mecca and each summer selected high school teachers made the pilgrimage. For six weeks the chosen were allowed access to the starry compound and later in colleagues' September accounts of trips and home improvement projects attend-ees would casually invoke the revered letters. JPL, the cerebral palace. Everyone in science, especially in greater L.A., desired a connection to Mecca. Bryer, who taught physics, and Wells, chemistry, had proudly done their stints.

A few years back the daughter of one of the project heads was on the *Roar* staff. A pleasant girl and clearly aware of her lineage. The father, an all around good fellow, worked the chains at the Friday-night games, served at the Boosters Annual Spaghetti Supper, and helped out at the Christmas Bazaar. Yet try as he might, in the end was the coda, shining neon – JPL. He knew it, they knew it. Anyone remotely connected with education understood well the unique terrain those creatures inhabited, so any attempt at everyman was doomed to failure. Reaching Mars would be less daunting.

Struck by the contrast between the hills behind, an immemorial geologic fence, and the tiny village below that saw the future, and speculating on a Devon, Evelyn JPL connection, Sloan missed his turnoff and exited at Sleepy Hollow Road, as rustic as its name implied. A row of pine trees exhaled their spiky greenness and he imagined himself a wooded existence.

After a tour of the neighborhood he eventually found the house, a two story Mediterranean with recessed windows. Directly across the street an English Tudor and further up California bungalows. Architectural schizophrenia. But that was L.A., mused Sloan. So many identities it didn't have one.

A half moon, cobbled drive led up to the Moorish, dark wood door. A Mercedes sedan and a BMW decorated the top of the moon. Sloan left the

Rabbit on the street and trudged up the drive. His reasoning that the curve might cause him to stall he knew was specious. Simple intimidation, that was all. He pressed the doorbell and listened to the reverberation of chimes.


"Granted, the Republicans have had the White House for two terms, and I concede we're going into a slow period, but I don't know that the Democrats can manage the economy," said Philip Loomis. He raised the martini glass and took a precise sip. "I think our fiscal problems are due in large part to a changing world." He was very white, with soft, alabaster hands culminating in finely trimmed, buffed nails. His hair, thin and silky receded dramatically, revealing a smooth, waxy paleness that melted into a benign face. One of those wrinkle-free cherubs of middle years. But for some puffiness beneath the eyes, no real signs of wear. A comfortable, well-fed product of order, of concise reports, of numbers precisely aligned, of lush-seated automobiles and climate control.

Sloan had always believed the man was merely the boy in hiding. When he was a kid the Loomises of the world were stationed in right field, if allowed to play at all. Always home by dark, always good grades. But the Loomises knew something he and his ilk didn't: the future would arrive, pragmatic and real. And when it came, the Loomises were ready.

"Only one man's opinion, but from my experience, if property values start to decline, and there's some sign of that, and unemployment goes up, I think we could be in for difficult times."

"Philly, that sounds so…so pessimistic." She touched her husband's arm and the fingers remained. A gesture of concern or a hint of what awaited? Sloan rejected the latter.

"I think it could, Joyce. Of course, I'm an accountant, not an economist."

"Does anyone really understand the economy. It's all so confusing." She threw up her hands and shifted her rump. With her ample, milky cleavage, she was her husband's counterpart. Both pleasantly inflated concoctions, all sugar and mild spice, nothing pungent. As the pre dinner conversation wore on, he realized they were childless, and kept having visions of the two of them rolling, panting, clutching, his wide, hairless belly jiggling above a bouncing erection, lost in her sponginess, desperately seeking entry and finally spilling its little self among the sheets.

"I think Phil's right, "said Montgomery. "From the commercial real estate side, I can tell you that values are starting to level off and the vacancy rate is up. And I'm with Phil on the coming election…I'm concerned about changing course, making substitutions. Seems to me you stick with your regular lineup. Take the ball and run with it. It's the bottom of the ninth. Go with what got you there." He crossed his legs, an edge of finality to the gesture, the tasseled Italian loafers underscoring his point. Even sitting, Montgomery looked tall and fit, but upright he was in fact imposing. And he found pretext to move about: to the bathroom, the kitchen, the game room to check on the kids. His was a rugged handsomeness, thick black hair, tinged with gray. A stellar jaw. Fine lines in a tanned brow suggested character, not worry. Grace the checker would be mad for him.

But Sloan suspected that Montgomery was, in the end, a pretender. His was a practiced masculinity, consciously constructed, artificial. In adolescence a hanger on. A talker. They would have tolerated him. He would have been useful with the girls, but in the end an amiable chicken shit. Adept at avoiding confrontation. Too pretty to get hit. If he ever gave you a reason, you'd eagerly kick his ass, but, of course, he never did.

That was it then, thought Sloan. When you were a kid it was all out there. Everyone knew where the other guy stood. No dissemblers. Phonies called to task. You backed it up, or shut up. But not in the adult future. And Montgomery too had apprenticed for those tomorrows, for that time when image would tell all.

Montgomery's wife was no less impressive, tall, athletic, broad shoulders, firm breasts, hair pulled back in a bun. Early forties, Sloan decided. Still only early spring, but the tan already a coffee ripeness, baked expertly, so as not to appear unnatural, the frosted lipstick completing the surf and sand look. He knew she would be stunning in a bikini. A seasoned Nordic, Newport goddess. They both played golf and tennis and swam. He had recently taken up racquetball, but Denise was reluctant.

"Monty loves it, but I just can't get into it. Doesn't appeal to me. I don't know why… I'm just not into it."

The BMW would be Monty's.

"It's not only the economy," offered Devon. "Don't you think the problems go much deeper, Monty? I mean the general state of things. Crime, education. Look at the school dropout rate. It's getting worse, not better."

"You're right. Absolutely. School is so important. Without a good education…in fact, Denise and I were just making that point to Starr. We had a long talk. We were very disappointed in her last report card. Far below her standards. We sat her down and spelled it out. I know she's only twelve, but Denise and I firmly believe that academics are priority one. She's crazy about soccer and swimming. A natural athlete, like her mother." Denise smiled demurely." But schoolwork comes first, right, Honey."

"Absolutely."

"Numero uno. Now Jasmine's fine, she's done well. Graduates next year. Same as Teddy…God how time flies. She's thinking Berkeley, but I think she's got a shot at Stanford. Who knows, she might just take after her old man – crimson and gold. Mighty Trojans. You only get one shot, though. Don't want to end up in the rough. Have to step up to the plate and take your best swing."

"Ian, I bet you could give us some interesting insights on the state of education," said Loomis. "Why do you think American kids aren't doing better?"

"It's a complex problem. Many variables," replied Sloan with deliberate obliqueness. Christ! He couldn't believe what he was saying. After all these years had he fallen under the spell of Stan Dugan, The Great Dane? Had he become one of them? Was that how he would end his days, part of officialdom, an in-service speaker? No, no…an aberration, not him…the company. Infectious. He had succumb to the disease. The bullshit disease.

"I don't know why our kids don't do better in international competitions. Something is definitely wrong."

"A lot of factors, I think. Work ethic, or lack of it. Home environment. Priorities. Education funding. Low standards – you name it." Despite himself, he was warming to the role.

"What do you teach?"

"English."

"Ever consider getting out of the classroom, Ian? Administration? Principal? Vice Principal?" said Devon. Was he taking a shot? Lack of ambition…that's why you lost your wife…no, he may not like the guy, but he wasn't nasty.

"Not really."

"A letters man, huh?" said Monty. "You look like the enemy – tell me you're not a Bruin."

"Cal State."

"Oh…Ev, do you think we could rustle up another Corona?"

"Yes, sure…Florinda." A sullen, overeweight Mexican woman of indeterminate age wearing an apron that read "Make My Day" emerged from the kitchen. "Another beer Florinda and some more chips." Florinda returned with the beer a and a bowl of the blue tortilla chips, set them on the table, and departed without giving any of them so much as a glance.

"Evelyn, these are delicious." Loomis scooped up a handful.

"I think you'll enjoy dinner. A recipe we discovered in Taos last summer. Mesquite chicken, with a twist. Florinda makes a wonderful version, with a little help from yours truly, so save room…Phil."

"Don't worry…I'm famished."

When they were ready to sit down, Evelyn asked Ian to get Teddy and the girls.

"I didn't tell him you were coming, so it will be a nice surprise."

Both Starr and Jasmine were Laura Ashley wrapped, femininity and wholesomeness apparently the desired effect. Another fraud, thought Ian. One glance at Jasmine and he had her pegged as the shorts and halter type on campus and he wondered who Monty and Denise were trying to impress with the "Little-House-on-the-Prairie" look? Evelyn and Devon? The Loomises? Certainly not him. Perhaps Teddy, who was struggling through a lifeless, monosyllabic exchange with Jasmine, while Starr, sprawled before the television, was engaged by the lovers' embrace.

"C'mon, everybody, dinner's ready. I'm Teddy's father and you must be Starr and Jasmine." The younger girl ignored him and Jasmine mumbled, "Hi."

"I hope you brought your appetite girls." He sensed his cheeriness as false as Jasmine's outfit.

"How's everything, Teddy?" He spoke softly as they followed the girls to the dining room.

"All right…I didn't know you were coming."

"Your mother thought we'd surprise you…school okay?"

"Yeah, why?"

"Just wondered how you were doing."

"Hurry up, you two," said Devon. "This is one hungry table."

The food was delicious, a marked improvement over Sloan's usual fare. He had been prepared for the healthful and tasteless or something so exotic as to be inedible but was pleasantly surprised and ate with zest, choosing to concentrate on his meal and listen rather than partici-pate. As the dinner progressed, he found himself studying Teddy and the girls. He had spent years observing teenagers, yet felt he didn't actually see them, or perhaps was simply tired of seeing them.

Then quite unexpectedly, but then revelations were like that he surmised, he saw Teddy anew, this boy opposite, his boy, his and the

73

woman at the end of the table. They had created him. Not willfully. Pure chance, nothing more. Even the circumstance was only partly of their making, the wine, the food… windows thrown open to the warm August night. And here he sat, fair skin, long, brown hair, deep blue eyes and a somber, dark expression.

The latent hostility of youth, chronic dissatisfaction, self loathing. Variations on a theme. Sloan had seen them all – there were just so many ways to twist a mouth, flare a nostril, fix a glare. Yet that same venom could transform summarily into hilarity, into real youth. He glanced faces in the quad at lunch he barely recognized later in the classroom.

Teddy had been…how had she put it…"the happiest little guy"? Why such anger and discontent in some but not in others? Sadness yes, at some time in all, but not hostility. and if he couldn't fathom why in them, they whom he saw daily, why would he have any more success with Teddy?

If Teddy was a portrait of restrained ire, Jasmine and Starr were a canvas of moroseness. The Sisters of Sullenness grunted when addressed and yawned unabashedly. No doubt the evening was an ordeal, but they could at least be civil. Despite their banter, he believed Monty and Denise were quite aware of their ill-mannered offspring, at least he hoped they were.

By meal's end and after several meaningful glances from Evelyn implying "time and tide wait for no man," Ian felt increasing pressure to seize the moment. But how, when? Like Huck he had embarked on this journey trusting only to chance, which, unlike Huck, was apparently deep-sixing him.

He savored the kiwi/raspberry tarts, maneuvering the last particles of the flaky crust down from his gums and teeth to the tip of his tongue to appreciate one last time before swallowing. And though the mission remained in limbo and he knew he should feel guilty, and he did, a little, he also knew he would never eat like this at home and the coffee was such a delicious blend.

Monty was discoursing on the strategies of net play, when Teddy slipped out of the room. Starr and Jasmine remained, the former on her back, her feet up on Evelyn's favorite wing chair, Laura Ashley having fallen ungracefully backward to expose plump thighs; the latter leafing through the current Cosmo the cover promising in large type "How To Please Your Man When It Counts."

Ian gestured to Devon and mouthed "bathroom," discreetly sliding from the chair, while Monty, in the center of the living room, angled his contoured body, positioning the imaginary racquet. Ian, moving unobtrusively behind the little group, should have anticipated Monty's peripheral vision.

"Ian, since you're up, a little assistance. Just for a moment." Before he could respond, Monty had him by the arm and stationed just forward of the coffee table.

"Remember, now, this is doubles. Ian is back approximately five feet or so. When you charge the net it's important not to commit too soon. That way your partner…"

Monty had moved on to the lob shot when Ian begged off the court and stepped silently down the hall.

The door was ajar. He hesitated. He couldn't smell anything. Yet a solitary joint would be near idyllic given his nightmare visions: Teddy bent over a table a straw up his nose, or worse, a tourniquet strangling his thin arm, a needle piercing the bulging vein. All the movie horrors and then some.

What he found was a reclining figure, earplugs in place, fingers keeping beat to a rhythm only he could hear.

"Teddy," he cried joyously. "Teddy." No response. He edged forward, his hand extended, a derelict gesture, somewhere between Tonto's greeting and a Crips salutation. Teddy jerked his head up startled and pulled out the earplugs.

"What is it?"

"Nothing. Just came to see how you're doing...Why did you leave? Are you okay?"

"Yeah. Why?"

"No reason."

"Are they gone yet?"

"No. And it's not polite to just get up and leave. Not when you have guests."

"Not my guests."

"Your father's guests then."

"Not my father."

"Your stepfather's ...anyway, you shouldn't abandon the girls like that." One minute he wanted to make him everyone's poster boy: "Drug-Free and Proud" the next he was reprimanding him.

"They're jerks."

"Don't say that."

"They are. Starr's a dumb little kid and Jasmine thinks she's great. All she does is talk about herself. Telling me all the great colleges she's going to apply to. Then she tells me her SAT score...What a joke. She doesn't have a clue."

"According to her father she gets good grades."

"Look what she takes. Anybody can get A's in easy classes."

"What about your college plans?"

"What about them?"

"Have you started thinking about where you want to go?"

"No."

"Don't you think you should?"

"What's the big deal? College is college." He replaced an earplug.

"That's not quite true."

"You're not exactly Mr. Harvard graduate."

"I didn't say I was...listen, put that away when I'm talking to you."

The boy responded to the command, like some primeval call from a time when they had roamed the landscape together. Ian moved to sit on the edge of the bed but Teddy quickly changed positions, his leg covering the spot. Ian retreated to the chair at the desk. "Your mother tells me you're not doing well at school. She says you don't study anymore, don't do your homework."

"Yeah?"

"She wants to know what's going on, what's bothering you. She says you don't talk to her anymore."

"So she goes running to you."

"Yes, she came to see me. Very upset. She's worried about you." Teddy smiled derisively and rolled his eyes. "She is...really concerned."

"The only thing she's 'concerned' about is her weight, if she can get reservations at some fancy restaurant or what she's going to wear..."

"You're being unfair."

"Aw, c'mon, Dad, you know how she is." The unexpected familiarity of the single-syllable warmth surprised him. A memory word. A holding of hands, rides on shoulders, games for two in unspoken joy. But that was gone and he no longer...still, he had uttered the word, so naturally. None of the usual awkward formality and distance of his infrequent visits.

"No one's perfect. Not me, not you, not your mother." He waited for agreement, pleased with himself. None came. "She tells me you quit the basketball team." Again silence. "Why? You always enjoyed basketball...varsity a lot tougher?"

"It's not that."

"She said you quit before the end of the season. When you were little I always told you never to quit once you started something."

"You did...so did she."

"It's not the same and you know it. You can't compare the two."

"Why not?"

"Because you can't. They're totally different." Teddy reached for the earplug. "Why did you quit."

"It's just not fun anymore." His voice rose. "Sure it's harder and I don't get as much playing time as I did on JV. But that's not why. I knew I wouldn't get to play much. It's just so…everyone treats it like it's life and death, especially the coach. Like we're big time college players or something. One kid was afraid to shoot because he knew if he missed Coach would be all over him. Even if he had an open shot most of the time he wouldn't take it and…he used to be a really good shooter. He could really stroke it. But the star of the team…he can do anything he wants. If he misses practice, no problem. He practically tells the coach what plays to run and we're all supposed to get him the ball. He takes almost all the shots. His father's always there, even at the practices. He wants Tyler to get a scholarship to UCLA or somewhere like that. So we all have to support him. It stinks! The coach doesn't care. He just wants to win. Get a college job, get ahead…grades the same way. Some kids are so crazy about getting good grades they'll do anything. Some of them cheat all the time."

"Don't you think you're exaggerating a little? Everyone who gets good grades cheats?"

"Most do…a lot of them. For some kids grades are the only thing that counts. Their parents put lots of pressure on… Berkeley, Harvard, somewhere like that. Yeah, they work hard but they'll cheat if they have to. And some of them, if they don't get an A, they complain to the teacher or their parents call and complain. They even call the principal. And most of the teachers give in. I know they do. They let them take tests over again or do extra credit or something. It sucks. You're a teacher. You know it's true."

"And you? What about your grades?" Teddy rolled over to face the wall. "I don't want to talk to the back of your head."

"I'm tired. I want to go to sleep."

"Listen…all right." He stood up and arched his back. How in God's name could anyone study in that torture seat. "Want the light out?" He stood waiting, his hand on the switch. The boy raised himself on one elbow, and looking over his shoulder said, "I'm not on drugs…never used drugs. A little beer at parties, but I never do drugs."

"Goodnight, Teddy." He turned off the light and closed the door a relieved and somewhat happy man.

After a quick word to Evelyn not to worry and a promise to call during the week, Ian attempted a speedy exit, but Monty would have none of it. Nearly a half hour later Sloan was still inching backward amidst the "so-nice-to-meet-yous" and "we'll-have-to-get-togethers." Monty kept his hand on Ian's shoulder insisting they play a few sets soon, though both knew they would never see one another again.

"Get you out of the chalk dust, away from the little devils. I think you'd enjoy it, Ian."

Sloan agreed to everything as he shuffled backwards, no longer really listening. If Monty had said "kiss my ass," he probably would have replied, "Yes, yes, soon. Very soon."

Outside at last, on the moonlit crescent, he made good his escape, casting last pleasantries as he faded into the darkness. He practically sprinted down the driveway, swaying from side to side as he fumbled for his cigarettes.

Twenty minutes later he remained, just south of their house, damning Wagner, bratwurst, Werner Hertzog, Gunter Grass…all that was German, even Ludwig. He stopped turning the ignition key. The incessant whining of the engine might draw them out and that's all he needed, a Monty treatise on the automobile. Or worse, the object of group pity. He sat smoking and contemplating his predicament, not even able to partake of the obligatory hood raising lest he draw attention. He took a deep drag and gave the key one last turn, willing the engine to catch as it struggled and strained, taunted until at last it tumbled Sisyphus-like and trailing off into obscurity.

Then the leave-taking began. He watched the ceremony unfold, much hugging and exclaiming and bursts of laughter. He was right. Monty's BMW led the way down the driveway. The headlights swung toward him and he ducked.

Near midnight having raised the hood and pulled on assorted cables to no avail he leaned back against the car and peered up at the Wallace household steeped in darkness and envied Devon and Evelyn tucked in, snug.

"Evening." The elderly man was wearing on of those newsboy's caps and walking a terrier. He peered at Sloan, sizing him up. The dog stretched on his leash did the same. He strained to get a good whiff of his pant leg.

"Hi."

"Won't start, huh?" Jesus Christ! Of course it wouldn't. Why the hell else would he be standing here in a strange neighborhood at this godforsaken time of night.

"Probably the battery." He stuck his head beneath the hood. "Try it again." Ian did as instructed. Barely a sound. Even Sisyphus had his limits.

"Okay...well, you wait here." Where the else would I go, thought Ian. "I'll be right back."

The good Samaritan returned with a new Volvo and jumper cable. The Rabbit started immediately. Sloan tried to assist with the removal of the cables but the old man was intent on doing it himself.

"I really appreciate this."

"My pleasure...my pleasure...Willis, stop that!" A fitting conclusion, thought Sloan. Above him Devon and Evelyn might at that very moment be making love, Devon humping away while Sloan's ankle was in turn subjected to the same.

"You can see the Little Dipper clear tonight." He was pointing up at the sky. "See it?"

"Yes…beautiful." He could not make out the pattern but in gratitude felt obliged to share the enthusiasm.

On the way back he promised himself, no more procrastinating, not putting it off to Spring Break. Monday he would take this piece of crap to the garage.

# NINE

He had once overheard another teacher in the faculty lounge refer to
him as a "straight arrow." Flattering, he supposesd, if the fellow meant
character, but he suspected he was referring to manner, appearance,
not an estimation of his moral state. There was no denying, he did look
the part. One of the few faculty who still wore a necktie. "Old fash-
ioned" would also suffice. He had begun his career wearing one and
did not abandon it as others did once they were tenured. The casual
look, informality, get closer to the students…none of it ever appealed
to him. As a result, with his short, graying hair, drab wardrobe and
unchic eyeglasses, he was easily placed in the "old" category by his
charges. And though 44 was indeed old to them, they had him teeter-
ing on dotage.

Ian was both amused and depressed by the subtle metamorphosis
in many of his fellows as they entered the middle years. They were the
mentors, "the guides," per Stan Dugan, the leaders, yet he saw in a sense
how they became the led. Slowly, incrementally, they began incorporating the students' language, a phrase here, an exclamation there,
those fragmented summations that explained everything and nothing. For some, even altering appearance. Two of the post forty males
had returned in September with little tufts of hair at the back of the

neck, nothing terribly noticeable, yet an undeniable homage to hipness. Another, a discreet earring.

Ian had long ago concluded that in no other field, save entertainment, which, depending on one's perspective, might readily define his profession now, were the players more conscious of aging. As they lost the untenured bounce in the step, grew heavier and grayer, and began taking their sick days, their clients remained sixteen. Time stood still on the other side of the desk. A world of youth that teachers could never quite enter; they could look, but not cross the threshold.

Away from campus, reality. On the street, in a mall, at a restaurant, and suddenly, "Mr. Sloan? Hi!" and the inevitable query: "Are you still teaching? You don't remember me, do you? Angela Capps... Period 5. I loved your class. You were my favorite teacher." Unable for a moment to respond, he stares, then a hint of something, her smile, a gesture perhaps, unchanged, harkens back, and like an "Our Town" production, the stage dim but for a single stream of muted light...a willowy figure in shorts and sweatshirt springs from her seat to pass out papers, happy to assist, to be of help.

A few pleasantries, that brief image, that backward glimpse and that young girl is gone, in her stead an overweight, thirtyish woman with sagging breasts and wide hips forced into denim that holds as best it can.

And modernity had crept into the classroom; teaching methodologies reflected the latest dictums: multiple intelligences, collaborative learning, cooperative learning, diversification, culturally based lesson plans. Increasingly out of step Sloan struggled to keep up. The lecture/ discussion, teacher-centered classroom was becoming passé. Or as the speaker at one of their in-services had declared, no more "sage on the stage." What bothered Ian the most, though, was the virus effect. Everyone bought in so readily. When Dugan had sounded a warning at the last faculty meeting – those unwilling to change would be left behind, his eyes rested on him a moment as they swept the room, and Ian imagined himself standing breathless in the rain as a yellow school bus, Dugan at the wheel, pulled out of the parking lot, the faculty waving to him from behind streaked glass.

He had never applied to be publications adviser. The position fell to him in his second year when Manuel, one of the custodians, found Ignatius, only a few years from retirement, slumped over his desk on a late May afternoon. A massive coronary, clutching a red pen in one hand and an essay in the other. The man's last concern on earth might very well have been an error in subject and verb agreement. Sloan never knew his surname, had only ever heard him addressed as "Ignatius," not "Iggy" or "Ig." Just Ignatius. All he knew for certain was he had inherited the adviser ship and within a few weeks marveled that old Ignatius had lasted as long as he had.

Having experienced only traditional classrooms, he was unprepared for the general chaos and struggled to adapt to a large industrial arts room partitioned by mere space, not even a portable sound wall, simply 35 desks aligned at the north end for his English classes. And his classes had always been conventional: assigned seating, no getting up without permission, the raising of hands. But publications students needed the freedom to converse, to move around, to leave the room even. He soon realized he could not keep tabs on everyone. He would have to trust them and that alone was frightening.

Then there was the telephone, both convenience and distraction. Archie the ad manager insisted he needed it to conduct business, including takeout orders at deadline time, and Sloan was still trying to determine who had made the long distance calls to Mammoth Lodge in February. He suspected Justin Baxter, but had no proof and Sloan still hadn't gotten around to grilling him. Under hard questioning most confessed.

And the untimely ringing drove him crazy. He might finally have his English students' interest, Grendel in a dripping, crimson fury stalking the darkened mead hall about to strike when interrupted by four per-sistent rings. A throaty female voice wanting to speak with "Archibald."

A golden, autumn afternoon in a New England wood, dappled sunlight filtering down through the trees to cover Hester and Arthur Dimmesdale reclining on the verdant earth, the more hormonal of the class suddenly awake. After all those years would there be an encore? Would Arthur finally pork her…again. And just then the ringing and even the horniest reverie interrupted. Wrong number. Oscar, from Plaza Interiors, wanting to come over that afternoon between one and four to lay, not Hester, but the new tile.

Yet he had reconciled himself to the turmoil of publications, the pendulum swing from dead time to deadline time, the oscillation from the languid to the frenetic. He was taking advantage of the former to prepare a test when Stephanie, Archie's assistant, sat down before his desk.

"Mr. Sloan, you have to help me." She was trying to frown, but when he smirked and without looking up said, "What's he done now?" her face exploded in unpracticed radiance.

"Mr. Sloan, don't laugh."

"I'm not laughing…"

"Yes, you are."

"Okay, what's wrong now?" He lay down the pen and removed his glasses, both annoyed and pleased at the interruption.

"Same as always, Mr. Sloan, only he's getting worse. He's crazy… He's making me crazy!"

"Your driving?" Stephanie not only sold the yearbook ads, but scheduled and supervised the photos using student models and Oliver Leary her photographer.

"Yes! Yes!" She dropped her head. "Oh, Mr. Sloan…what am I going to do?"

"I told you before – just ignore him."

"As soon as he gets in the car he starts…and he can't even drive himself! He's always telling me to watch my left, watch my right, don't forget to signal. I'm going too fast, I'm going too slow..oh, Mr. Sloan," she pleaded her eyes brilliant and unable to keep from laughing at his amused expression. "Mr. Sloan! I'm serious! He's even getting after me about my parking. Do you know what he did yesterday?"

"I can't imagine."

"I was starting to parallel park in front of Walker's Pharmacy. Hardly any traffic. No problem, right? Then without saying a word he jumps out of the car and starts giving me directions, standing on the sidewalk waving his hands back and forth like a freak. Mr. Sloan, I was so embarrassed. I can't stand it anymore."

"Have you ever considered that maybe it's just his way of showing affection?"

"Oh, puleazzz. Oliver? Look at him. Does that look like someone capable of affection?" She nodded toward a slight boy in black t-shirt with white lettering: "I'm just visiting your planet" sitting on the floor in the corner, legs outstretched, eyeglasses in his lap and a camera lens protruding from his chest. "Are we talking about the same Oliver Leary?"

"Maybe you're just not seeing him clearly."

"Mr. Sloan, look at him,. He's a geek!"

"Stephanie, be kind. Something might be bothering him."

"Not 'something.' Everything. He's crazy!"

"He's probably just depressed. Wasn't there some trouble with his girlfriend?"

"Yes…oh, Mr. Sloan, do you know what she did?" A cautious glance backward before pulling her chair closer.

"No, but I'm sure you're going to tell me."

"She left everything he gave her, all the stuff, letters, jewelry, every-thing, in a shopping bag in front of his locker. When he came to school on Monday, there it was. All the stuff, all his gifts. It's so sad."

"Well, there your are, see. No wonder he's depressed. You should be understanding, kind. Make allowances for him."

"Mr. Sloan, I am. I tried to talk to him about it. I said it was terrible what she did but he just told me to concentrate on my driving."

"He's only concerned for your welfare…in fact, you might be the cause of the breakup."

"Mr. Sloan, don't mock me."

"All right. All right…just remember, Oliver's a unique case."

"He's making me crazy!" She tried again for distraught, but when he grinned, she threw up her hands. "Mr. Sloannnn."

"Okay. Okay. I'll talk to him."


Near the end of the period, following an understanding of sorts between Stephanie and Oliver, Julie approached, envelope in hand. He braced himself, but the vein was still blue, still intact.

"I got Mr. Roth's letter. Do you want to read it?"

"Let's take a look."

"He can't spell 'holocaust,'" she added. "He's got two l's."

"Well…you know history teachers. Only concerned about the big issues; spelling's beneath them." Not even the hint of a smile. She watched him intently as he read. "Pretty much what he told me."

"Do you think we should run it?"

"Up to you. Your page and you're the editor-in-chief. I implied that we would. But it's your decision…something wrong?"

"No, but…"

"What?"

"I don't want anyone…Some people might think he's racist or anti Semitic or…but he's not, I know he's not."

88

"Actually, I mentioned that to him, but he was only concerned that we might get in trouble."

"We don't care about that." Her voice rose, a quivering below the eye. He wanted to point out that her part of the "we" would be leaving in June.

"Do you think he makes a valid point?"

"Yes, Mr. Sloan. He's right. But it doesn't matter whether we agree or not."

"Okay, go ahead then." My God, it was like a movie. He could see the title: "The Truth at All Costs," "A Mentor and His Disciples." No. "Deluded Teacher, Misguided Staff."

She started from the desk in triumph, then swung around. The vein had settled.

"Mr. Sloan, thanks again for the recommendation. I got in. I got my acceptance letter from Northwestern yesterday." She smiled sweetly, made all the lovelier for its rarity. The door had opened briefly and he caught a glimpse of the girl only.

"Congratulations. That's wonderful. Your parents must be very happy."

"Not really."

"Why?…What do you mean?"

"They're kind of…They're not too thrilled about me wanting to be a journalist. They think journalism's more for men…plus it doesn't pay very well."

"That's probably true…"

"They say I'll have a better life doing something else."

"Give them time. They'll come around."

"I doubt it."

# TEN

"Help yourself to snacks." Stiffle pointed at the two desks drawn
together in the corner of his room, with its bank of windows that provided a panoramic view of the quad, the center of the campus. If the
venetian blinds were open, the late afternoon meeting might attract the
occasional loiterer hoping to catch a glimpse of teachers at their ease,
their guard down. Perhaps a respected personage picking his/her nose
or the scratching of an ass, something to take back for the next day's
lunch time amusement.

When Bengstrom arrived he assumed his enthusiasm, his buoyant
spirits would transform the faculty with a zeal to serve. Anticipating
fierce competition, the principal developed an elaborate application
for department-head positions which he placed strategically around the
faculty lounge. Only a few were ever submitted and those by administrator wanna-bes. None from the English Department, which had its
own system of rotating Chairs, each member, except Ian, serving two-
year stints. He had somehow managed to avoid his turn. Not that he was
lazy or irresponsible; at least that's what he told himself. He simply had
no patience for it, no belief. It just seemed futile. He might yet have to
resign himself to the inevitable. Sniffle's term was up in June, and since

Gerald Cruz was new to the department and given a bye, he remained the logical choice.

Much to the Great Dane's chagrin, the intense rivalries he had envisioned never materialized, his prized packets ultimately serving as placemats for the annual Christmas brunch.

All but Vivian Shelby, star of the department, and Ian, went for the peanut brittle, bran muffins, and room temperature Diet Coke. Horses to a trough thought Sloan; put it out, they'd eat it. Teachers were the ones who hung about the sample tables in supermarkets hoping for seconds.

Vivian, quintessentially feminine, with a gentle, yet condescending smile, the kind bestowed on children who might be amusing, clever even, yet still children, still of the lower order, sat in dignified silence. A Stanford alum, she wore her mantle of complacency well. Ian decided that it must be wonderful to live without doubt. She taught seniors only – both Honors and Advanced Placement – and was adjudged the scholar of the department, her opinions on all matters academic valued above all others. She traversed a path above the rough edges of campus life. No one would dare request she chaperone a dance or advise a club. Administrators over the years were all but apologetic in the requisite evaluation process. Bengstrom referred to her as Lady Vivian, in jest, but only partly. Clearly, he was smitten with the Grand Dame. In her presence he seemed so intimidated, one expected him to genuflect and kiss her hand.

A simple dresser who, though capable of deep greens, navies, and earth tones in season, was best suited to the softer hues, whites, creamy beiges, gentle pastels. The Queen Mum School. An ephemeral, talcumy presence. An immaculateness, a wispiness that bespoke pale moonlight and veils and mists. Guinevere, Sir Gawain. Discreetness, adoration and scented phrases. How then, he wondered, did she handle the bawdiness of Chaucer or even Shakespeare? Probably best left to silent reading where they would remain undiscussed. Hard to believe she had three children. He couldn't imagine her actually having sex. The sight of a cock? Foreplay? Impossible. A sonnet or two perhaps, before disrobing. Then a gentle, accidental coupling in the dark, blindfolded.

Vivian's classroom mirrored her refinement. Exquisite water prints of her deities in tasteful frames – Keats, Shelley, Byron, Yeats and, of course, the Bard. She was passionate, but artfully so. When she was younger, her best and brightest made their pilgrimages to her enchanting, wisteria draped sanctuary with its half-acre garden. A refuge in companionable nature, a respite from coarseness. And there, in that bygone time, they sent pentameters heavenward, drawing their evenings to a close with tea and cakes on the patio, the strains of Debussy, Liszt, Grieg, wafting through the French windows to infuse the falling night.

But now, after 36 years and facing an audience of body piercers, green hair and Sex-Wax t-shirts, romance was on the wane, and she too seemed to settle for simply getting through the day. Retirement would be welcomed. A successful husband, accomplished children. Another tour of the continent, but autumn this time; no more sweaty summer masses of semi literate mid western housewives or the Asian hoards with their ubiquitous cameras. Galleries, museums, theaters, where one could mingle with one's own in London's deep November. In a short while, such would be hers. In a few weeks down would come the prints, the posters, the bust of Shakespeare and she would depart Room 8 for the last time.

"And she's only a freshman! Can you imagine!" said Marcia Trollop Nazar, soon-to-be, significant literary figure. On the verge, on the very precipice of discovery, according to her accounts of those who had read her work at the various summer writing programs she attended. Marcia was committed to the creative process, her constant companion a small black notebook wherein she jotted, everyone assumed, penetrating observations, insightful conclusions, which in time would culminate in an accomplished piece.

"Astonishing." Vivian touched her throat, a sedate gesture.

"Three months gone and she's starting to show. Her mother wants me to provide detailed lesson plans for next September, October, and November."

"The child is due in November?"

"Around Thanksgiving. Something to be thankful for, huh?" Marcia crossed her athletic legs. Ian appreciated her firm thighs, but she did not appreciate his appreciation and recrossed in the opposite direction. She was attractive in a rough sort of way.

"Incomprehensible," added Vivian, now examining her blouse buttons, wishing belatedly for a higher neckline, but it had been so unseasonably warm.

Marcia got up for another bran muffin, and Ian followed the sway of her well-rounded, compact ass. She bicycled on weekends and occasionally to school; he could imagine those ripe buttocks, more shapely even, in tight, black riding pants, perched atop the small leather seat. Definitely an erotic sports connection. Alpine skiing, Marcia unpeeling before a cozy fire, the glow highlighting the curves of her body. Or big game hunting. Sweaty passion, naked under canvas on the Serengeti, the wild animal cries, hers and theirs. A Devaney interlude if there ever was one.

About the same age as Sloan, was their Hemingway aficionado. He hunted and fished and a few years back had run with the bulls in Pamplona breaking his arm in three places. He wore turtleneck sweaters, even on warm days, and had cultivated an impressively thick, dark moustache and developed, over time, a throaty laugh and was given to abstract pronouncements on pain, suffering, and futility. But Devaney was married and Marcia had her roommate Delores, who was a nurse and her riding partner. Kirk in math saw them once, peddling effortlessly down Santa Monica Boulevard in West Hollywood on a two-seater.

When she first joined the staff there had been plenty of interest, but her admirers soon realized that Marcia was spoken for.

"I don't understand what these kids are thinking about," said Stiffle. "If they can't control themselves, you'd think they would take precautions."

"Some things are not so easily controlled," said Devaney, hinting at much.

"I don't know," said Sloan. "Seems pretty simple to me. Zip up, or cover up." Vivian frowned. "Got that Gerald?"

Gerald Cruz wrote down everything in neat script at both department and faculty meetings. No one took notes at department meetings, except Stiffle, and those merely bulleted lists. Anything important would be restated in a later in a follow-up memo. But Gerald wished to impress. Being Hispanic, he'd be on the fast track and out of the classroom in four or five years max. Yes, Gerald was definitely administrator material.

"I mean, Ian," said Devaney squaring his shoulders, jaw firmly set. Even in his lousy shape Ian knew he could kick his ass. If necessary, kick him in the balls. No, not a good move. *The Sun Also Rises*. Devaney/Jake Barnes? The prospect was disturbing, "passion is more than sex."

"I should say," intoned Vivian. "But I hardly think these children know much of true passion."

"No big mystery," said Ian. "They want to get a little and are not willing to wait as long as we did."

Turning her back on him completely, Vivian said, "You have a way of reducing everything to its most elemental."

"Conciseness," said Sloan, "the essence of good writing. Isn't that what we always tell them. Use only what you need."

"Yes, and appropriate diction. Seek to elevate, not demean," countered Vivian. In deference to the impending retirement, he allowed her the last word.

"Open House after Spring Break," said Stiffle Everybody ready?"

"Ready as we'll ever be," said Marcia, not looking up.

"I assured Bengstrom we would have samples of student work on display. But don't have any grades on them. Textbooks, the usual. And don't get involved with parents about their kid's grade. If they want to talk about that, tell them to make an appointment for a conference. Bengstgrom wants us in the auditorium by seven. The first ten rows on the north side are for faculty. Sharon will have the choir in the quad at 6:30 and throughout the evening. They're doing show tunes. She calls it her 'Broadway Extravaganza.'"

"Anybody know anything about Bengstrom? Is he coming back?" said Marcia. She had drawn her effort to a close and put away the note-book with an air of satisfaction. They had her full attention.

"Haven't heard a thing," said Stiffle..

"Notice how he stays in his office all the time now with the door closed," added Devaney. "No more open-door policy. Remember when he started he said his door would always be open. He'd always be accessible."

They droned on about textbooks and fall assignments and Sloan felt himself sinking under the weight of their voices. Prufrock had nothing on him. But rather than his own life, he was dissecting theirs. In ten years Marcia's thighs would be losing the battle of cellulite, her breasts would have fallen, but she and her companion or another, Delores sub-stitute, would still pedal the boulevard, though less vigorously. And Devaney, with salt and pepper beard, would have slipped comfortably into the Papa role and speak even more obscurely of pain and suffering. And Gerald would have long since put away his pencil and abandoned the classroom for a vice-principalship. Stiffle retired. And Vivian. She would have entered the realm of the aged, and in her twilight, still cultured, still superior as she stepped judiciously among the lavender and flax whispering Keats and Shelley and recalling former adoration.

Sloan wished to throw a rock into their pond, watch them scatter, upend them. And he? Where would he be at 54? Not here, he decided. He would pull himself out; better to perish gasping than surrender to the depths. He would never serve his term as chair.

"Vivian, are you feeling nostalgic?" said Stiffle. "Your last Open House. Do you think you'll miss old AHS?"

Vivian offered a benign face. "When James and I were dining last evening, he asked that very question. I did not know quite how to respond. I think one just continues on, doesn't one? But yes, I suppose before long I shall feel somewhat nostalgic."

# ELEVEN

Spring Break. An unseasonably warm evening. The Rabbit had been repaired, faulty fuel injectors, but on this night he would be on foot. After dinner a sudden, inexplicable urge to walk, though he was not, by nature, a walker. Perhaps the balmy weather or the melancholy that had unaccountably taken hold. Whatever the reason, he found himself on the sidewalk outside his building in a quandary – right, or left? He had no destination, nowhere in particular he wanted to go; then he thought of the bridge. About two miles. Not a great challenge to many, but to Sloan, for whom all exercise was exertion of the last resort, the trek would be formidable.

He began briskly, then realizing there was no hurry, no class to meet, no deadline to make, slowed his pace to savor the evening. Other strollers gave pleasant greetings, a word or two, or simply the knowing smile of shared experience as they passed. He began to see his neighborhood differently, seeing it for the first time really. He peered down driveways into backyards, took in the sweep of verandas and, though told as a child it was rude to do so, glanced into the living room windows he passed. He knew he was being intrusive, but the impulse was too strong.

Some rooms were attractive, warm and inviting, others spare and cold, dull, somber, foreboding even. Still others, cluttered, confused, garish. A woman about to draw curtains glared at him and Ian quickly looked away. What was he searching for? What was he expecting to see with these glimpses into other lives? Perhaps his own, his prior life: the yard, the small garden, the going inside, the Saturday dinners? Those little portions of companionable existence.

Down Colorado, then the incline. Nearly a half mile to the summit. He wavered, yet was determined to stand on the bridge at night, certain his effort would be rewarded. Something beautiful, something magical, some wonderful moment awaited.

A young couple holding hands was descending, pulled by joy and gravity. Absorbed in each other, they passed oblivious of him. In the fading light her slender arm swung gracefully and an image from his own youth returned. Late spring his senior year, an evening not unlike this one. The departing of adolescence, a time of keen senses and expectation. A fragrant, humid night, yet a cooling breeze that lapped against them as they stood within the sphere of a streetlight waiting for the bus, holding hands, not speaking, steeped in that velvet moment. A blue and white floral print, a thin strap over each shoulder. The glow, flecked by the shadows from the shifting leaves of the tree behind danced on the fine curve of her arm and shoulder and he wished only that the bus might never arrive.

When he finally reached the bridge, Ian was exhausted and breathing heavily. Not a good sign. He must get more exercise. He struggled to the first niche and flopped down beneath an ornate lamp. Indentures, like side altars, with a concrete slab on which two could sit comfortably, dotted both sides of the bridge. Above each alcove a brilliant globe, a chapel of light.

His breathing normal again, Sloan stood and gazed down into the arroyo. Darkness ushered out what remained of the twilight blue, the cliffside trees black sentries, the ravine an inky depth. He lit a cigarette and knew the climb had been worth it. He would pause at each tabernacle to peer beyond the railing and make his offering, his appreciation, his Stations of the Cross as the nuns had instructed on Good Fridays all those years ago.

The bridge followed a distinct curve midway across, so pronounced that half a span behind a driver lost sight of the car ahead. A figure appeared in the distance, a man carrying a suitcase. A pronounced step, purposeful. As his fellow pilgrim drew near, he saw the bag was cheap and battered, the clothes baggy and worn. Onward he came, paying him no heed and as they drew parallel, Ian glanced at the stubbled face, the frozen expression. He wanted to offer a greeting to acknowledge a kindred soul, a fellow wanderer, but their eyes did not meet. The stranger stepped past, head aloof, a face not of torment, but disdain almost. Ian turned and watched the receding traveler meld into the winding sidewalk and the night. Why had he not spoken to him? Was he afraid he would ask for money? And what if he had? Where was he going? Had he real business? Something of import, something that needed taking care of? Or was he merely walking the time away? Better an imagined destination than none at all.

Having four times paid homage to beauty, Sloan came upon a car parked opposite, tight against the curb. The hood was not up and no emergency lights, no one, nothing. Simply there. Abandoned, half way across the bridge. No, there was movement inside the car, a head bobbing up and down, a child, now you see me, now you don't. Whoever it was had not yet seen him. Retreat beckoned, the sooner the better. Enough of nature for one night. He deciphered a woman crouched by the rear wheel and was torn. He went a little further on to get a closer look. Surely someone would stop, provided she wasn't rearended first. While he was weighing chivalry against flight, with a finger on the latter, he was startled by the sound of his name.

"Mr. Sloan, hi." He hoped to God it was not a former student. She had come out from behind the car and was waving to him. Grace the cashier was had come to meet him, standing in the center of the road, smiling and Sloan had an overwhelming urge to leap over the railing. Suicide Bridge. Apropos.

Instead, Ian Sloan, sojourner on a lovely evening, wanting nothing more than a Walden moment, a spiritual commune with nature, found himself cautiously approaching an old Saab, which had once been a tomato red but had since darkened beyond mere vino to a dull, mud maroon. A vehicle that belonged in a desert where disturbed men with assault weapons prepared for the last battle.

"Flat tire?" The inside rear end was only slightly jacked up.

"Yeah, can you believe it?" Given the condition of the car, he could, easily.

"You better turn on your emergency lights. This is a dangerous spot. Cars can't see you until they're practically on top of you."

"They don't work."

"Lets hurry and get it changed." She had begun removing the nuts and had been struggling with the last two when he came along. He threw his weight upon the tire iron and strained. Neither budged.

"Those suckers are really on tight,"

"Garages," he gasped, "tighten with those power guns. Sometimes they don't realize…got it! There's one." Without looking he handed her the nut. When she received it, she let her fingers slide down his palm.

"Take a minute to catch your breath," she said.

"Sooner you get out of here, the better." He locked the tire iron on the last and pushed with all his weight. Nothing.

"Let me help." She squatted next to him, and before he could respond had gripped the iron. "Okay, let's do it together – one, two, three." And just as they pushed down in unison, a blinding burst of light, a screech of tires and he braced for the impact. So this was how it would

102

end. In an instant he saw his mangled body splattered upon the bridge, Grace lying next to him. The *Roar's* headline: "United in Death: a Bridge Tragedy." The school would declare a day of mourning, and Bengstrom would address staff and students in somber tones at a special assembly. Perhaps a reading by Vivian, a few lines from *Romeo and Juliet*. No, that was a stretch. She'd never consent. Anyway something good would come of it – relief for those students who had yet to complete the reading for their book report.

The driver swerved, careening onto the sidewalk opposite before righting himself.

"Asseholes!" a boy hollered as the car sped off. Grace dashed to the front of the Saab, her arm extended, the thick, middle finger jabbing the night.

"Fuck you, Dude!" She returned panting. Sloan's face was wet and he too was gasping.

"That was close. C'mon, let's get this changed." His hands shook as he inserted the iron again and they both pushed down.

"See! We got it! We make a good team." She grinned at him and twirled the iron until the wheel hung loose. He grasped the tire, determined to go it alone, and the tendon in his arm fluttered as he pulled the wheel free.

"Mommy." The window was down and the little head hovered above Sloan.

"Everything's okay, Honey. Go back to sleep."

"Who that?" The child yawned and drooled.

"A nice man who's helping mommy…now, go back to sleep."

She had already removed the bald spare from the trunk and crouched to help him align the holes. The third button of her Western blouse was undone and she was not wearing a bra. He was certain it had been buttoned earlier. He was placing the flat in the trunk when another set of headlights appeared and he froze. The car slowed and passed cautiously without comment.

"You better get going."

"Where's your car?"

"I'm walking."

"No you're not! Get in."

"No, really. It's okay. I'm fine."

"I'm not gonna let you walk back...Get in." He felt too tired to resist and was not about to stand there debating the issue. He had been lucky twice; he did not wish to tempt fate a third time.

"How do you like your Saab?" Christ! What a fool. Might as well ask a cripple how he liked his wheelchair. But if he controlled the conversation, kept it on trivialities he might avoid any further entanglement. The boy was stretched out on the back seat, eyes open, sucking his thumb and playing with his bellybutton.

"It runs. Car's a car with me. I got it cheap from my girlfriend's brother. He gave me a great deal. Course he thought he was gonna get somethin' extra. Know what I mean?" She gave him a long look, her lips parted and he felt both repelled and fascinated.

"I see."

"No way, Jose. Not this girl. I don't just throw it around." He watched the thick denim leg work the clutch as she shifted gears.

"That spare's in pretty bad shape. I wouldn't use it too long."

"Yeah, I know. Whole car's in bad shape...what do you drive? Wait! Don't tell me...Buick, right?"

"No."

"Oldsmobile?"

"Volkswagen."

"VW." She laughed. "Wow, I never would have figured that."

"Why not?"

"Well...you know. I mean...older guys..." He let her struggle. "My ex- boyfriend Armand, Ben's father, he had a '68 Bug. He was a wild man, but he kept that car in mint condition. He's had lots of offers for it, but he won't sell. He'll never sell that car. He'd be miserable without it. He loves that baby. You got a Bug?"

"Rabbit."

"Hey, Ben," she called to the slobberer behind. "Mr. Sloan's got a rabbit too." Ben gurgled his approval.

"You smoke?" She reached for the generic brand cigarette pack on the dash. A gaping figure fissure revealing foam rubber ran outward from the windshield across the dry, brittle surface.

"Yes."

"Here." She took one and offered him the pack.

"Maybe we shouldn't…with Ben…"

"Oh, Ben, he don't mind. You don't mind if Mommy has a smoke, do you, Ben?" A satisfied chortle in the darkness. "See."

"How old is Ben?" At the sound of his name, Ben giggled a response.

"Almost three, aren't you Big Fella?" Silence. He clearly preferred his given name. She fumbled with the matches and the care started drifting. Sloan felt his legs tighten and he gripped the door handle. To escape the bridge not once, but twice, only to die in a bloody, head-on collision. And such a promising start, such a nice evening, uncomplicated; now here he was trapped in a deathmobile with this creature and her offspring. The safety of his little apartment, his sanctuary, seemed a distant dream. A long bath. He was an undemanding person…a simple request by most standards. Might the gods at least grant him that.

"Here, let me."

Her eyes wistful above the flame as she leaned toward him suggested more than he cared to fathom. Had he by this seemingly ordinary gesture, unbeknownst to him breached some sacred boundary? A cultural rite that he would only be made privy to after the compact was sealed? The decree issued? Did the lighting of a woman's cigarette at night in a battered Saab signify betrothal? An ancient gypsy ritual sworn in blood. Was that his future then? Grace or escape, forever on the run, pursued by dark, bandana headed, wild-eyed men with gold earrings and curved daggers in their belt.

"Thank you, Mr…wait a minute. This isn't fair. You know my first name but I don't know yours. I only remember your last name…from your checks. I only look at last names because management told us customers will feel good, you know, flattered, if you call them by name. Especially the regulars, like you. But I can't keep calling you 'Mr. Sloan' now that we're friends and all." The "and all" sounded ominous.

"Ian."

"That's so…so…Ian. I like it. Sounds very classy…very intellectual. Guess that's why you're a teacher." He popped the spring of the overflowing ashtray and a Mt. Vesuvius of ash and butts rained down on them.

"Sorry."

"That's okay. I hardly ever empty it. I'm a slob." The lipstick stained filters and the rank nicotine stench prompted a silent pledge though he knew he wouldn't keep it. "Cigarettes are getting so expensive. That's why I switched to generics. They're not bad. Try one." She offered the pack.

"No thanks…I've got a sore throat."

"You gotta economize these…You taking anything? We got lots of stuff reduced, you know, cough medicine, Tylenol…all that stuff."

They drove on in a conscious silence, that hanging presence that reminded him of the confessional when he was a child. Those agonizing Friday revelations. The door across the screen would slide back so deliberately you could hear each centimeter of progress and the figure opposite, in the shadows, waiting. The nuns would dismiss class early after lunch and march them across the street to the empty cathedral. Both blessing and curse: brief freedom then the agony of guilt.

One Friday in late autumn as they approached the doors two by two, the boy behind nudged him and he looked to see a dog humping another on the plot of grass by the steps. The boys snickered and

106

elbowed each other. The girls, except a few of the more daring, looked away, while the nuns gazed heavenward. He knew they had seen.

Crossing an intersection near his street, Grace caught him evaluating her breasts outlined in the oncoming headlights. She smiled and to his surprise he felt himself aroused. He tried to imagine her unclothed. He had never made love to a heavy woman.

"Tell me where to turn."

"Huh? Oh…just let me off at the next corner."

"Are you sure? I can take you…"

"No…No…this is fine." She eased over to the curb and he was pulling up the handle before she had come to a complete stop. The door wouldn't open.

"Sometimes it sticks." She reached across, pressing her breast against his arm. "And you have to jerk it…like that."

"Thanks for the ride." He lowered his head to the open window, "Would have been a long walk …well, take care." The urge to run was so strong it required a deliberate effort to step casually from the car.

"Ian Sloan." He froze. One of the nuns…the miscreant, the boy caught eyeing the dogs on the church grass. "You're not gonna get away just like that." Her voice kept him rooted. "Ben and me," no sound from the rear. Ben was sleeping. Lucky Ben. "want to show our appreciation. You been a real lifesaver."

"No, really…"

"Yes 'really.'" She ran her probing fingers along the back of the seat, still warm from his body, and plunged them into the crevice. Retrieving a pencil stub, she scribbled on the inside of a matchbook cover. "Ben and me want you to come to dinner. Here's my address. I'm only a block from the store. You wouldn't think so, white bread like me, but I make the best tamale pie and enchiladas you ever ate. Good as anything you can get in East L.A. All my Mexican friends say I'm a great cook. Friday night I work, so let's make it Saturday, about seven."

"I...I can't make it Saturday. I'm..."

"Okay, Sunday then. No excuses. I won't take 'no' for an answer." She handed him the matchbook and shifted into gear "104D Burkitt... Don't forget, Sunday, around seven. You like Mexican, don't you?"

"Yes...Mexican's good."

"Great! See you then."

He put the matchbook in his pocket. He knew she was watching him in the rear view mirror.

# TWELVE

"This high enough, Mr. Sloan?" Thurman steadied himself on the counter in the journalism room. "You want it a little lower?"

"That's good." Mid April, deadline day and a 3" block of white on page nine in Features. The work order on the flagholder was submitted before Thanksgiving. Typically AHS. Delay it, forget it, lose it. And if processed, proceed at the most inconvenient time.

"Old Glory," uttered Thurman as he pressed the bracket into the wall. He leapt from the counter. "Old Glory," he repeated, trying to catch his breath. "They sure don't give her the respect anymore, do they?" The custodian shook his head sadly. He had thinning curly hair and a handlebar moustache, both dyed a rust brown. He was in his mid fifties and wished he were not. Each year he participated in Anesthesia's 10K Community Run and had yet to finish one. He ate power bars, drank juices, and worked out, after a fashion. Still the leanness and meanness eluded him. Everyone loved him in a brotherly way, but Thurman, twice married, one divorce, one disappearance – she went to the kitchen in the dead of night for a glass of milk never to return, no trace, save a depleted checking account – wanted more than brotherly love. Ever the optimist, he had recently joined a fitness center, hoping that among the machines and the camaraderie he might meet that special someone. Of that complexity called "woman" he believed he had learned much. "They're impossible," he had once told Ian. "Can't live with 'em, can't live without 'em."

"The Sixties did it, don't you think, Mr. Sloan?" He was on a first-name basis with everyone else, but Ian was always "Mister Sloan."

"Ah…yes."

"All the demonstrations and everything. I'm not saying the war was good…I don't know your politics, but Old Glory took it on the chin. Don't you think?"

"Yes…yes, he did."

"We're about the same age. We remember when she was treated better, don't we?"

"Yeah, we sure do…that's perfect, Thurman. I'll get one of the students to replace the flag. You don't have to bother. Thanks a lot."


"Mr. Roth is having second thoughts," said Julie. "He talked to me after class yesterday. I think he's afraid we might get into trouble."

"What'd you tell him?"

"I said we stand behind our letter policy," she replied with the firmness and clarity of the righteous. Roth's missive would be posted alongside the only other letter they had received, a student complaint, riddled with grammatical errors, about the increase in athletic fees, from a boy whose father was a six-figure executive of a major company. Julie would position both beneath her Perspective column, topic: "Ethnic Clubs – Why They Do More Harm Than Good." Great. He would never leave this place alive. Assassinated in the faculty parking lot by a Chinese, Hassidic Jew from Uganda.

Since she had joined the staff and declared war on equanimity, his editor-in-chief had managed to alienate both district and site administration, various alumni, a select core of teachers, and the PTA. Who was left? Thurman?

"You know, it would be nice if we could put something positive in these pages once in a while." Again, his words sounded eerily familiar. Was he too of Scandinavian lineage? Bengstrom "The Great Dane" he "The Surly Swede." "Maybe a tribute to someone, a club or something. Anything. Something positive for a change."

"We have the 'Yeas' and 'Nays.'"

"I mean a full length editorial actually praising someone or something." She searched his face, scrutinizing him as a witness might a suspect in a lineup.

"Mr. Sloan, it's not a booster page; it's an editorial page."

"I realize that, but there must be something good going on around here." Her righteous indignation occasionally got on his nerves. "Anyway, you need a filler in Features – page nine. Maybe a puzzler of some kind." He could suggest one: Name the Teacher – Which of the following goes by the moniker "The Outcast"? A. Mr. Sloan B. Ian Sloan C. Sloan D. all of the above." Except for the typos I've marked, everything's fine."

"I think Stanley has a problem with the proofreading. I meant to talk to you about it …I have to read everything again to catch what he missed."

"He's just not paying attention…tell him to shape up. Tell him I said his grade depends on his correcting all the errors. That's his job."

"It's kind of not his fault."

"Why not? He's the proofreader."

"Stanley thinks he might be dyslexic. His mother's going to get him tested next week."

"Great! A dyslexic proofreader. When did you find this out?"

"I kind of thought there was something wrong. I tried to talk to him after the last issue but…Stanley's very sensitive. I'll just have to make sure I read everything after he's done."

"How can you? You won't have time."

"I'll make some of the deadlines earlier. It'll be okay."

"Mr. Sloan, call for you." Archie yelled from the doorway of what he liked to think of as his "office," but which, in fact, was a storeroom, leaving Thurman with just as much a claim since he had kept his mops and brooms there for years. Above an empty cleaning supplies box that served as his desk Archie had posted, "All The Bucks Stop Here."

Ian seldom used the phone and had only ever received one call, from an irate parent who had bullied Martha, Bengstrom's secretary, into providing the number. And the only person he had ever given it to was his father.

"Archie, if you don't mind." The ad manager loitered by the doorway, reluctant to surrender his "office."

"You won't be too long, will you? I have some important calls to make."

"Important calls?" Was he delusional? Sidney's Lock and Key? Same ad, same size, same page for God knows how many years, long before he had taken over the *Roar*. The check in the same amount always arrived at the same time – one week after publication, and though they had the occasional deadbeat, Sidney's was the typical account. And it was highly doubtful any of the merchants actually believed that advertising in the *Roar* would increase business. The ads were simply a way to support the publication without treating it as a charity. Their own phone line, rather than a necessity, was more a concession to Archie's ego and a gesture to show Sloan trusted him, considered his position essential, but he had inadvertently created a monster – the best laid plans.

"Close the door, Archie…Yes, this is Ian Sloan…no, not Alan, Ian… I-A-N. Yes, Ian…Yes, I'm his…yes, my father." He had met Dr. Tsai once and had no trouble communicating, but his receptionist was nearly incomprehensible. "'Stars how'? I don't understand. 'Heart his alm and wibs'?" After much straining and repetition he learned the old man had fallen down the stairs at the hotel and hurt his arms and ribs, but nothing broken.

Over the years his father had gone through a legion of medical personnel, with stays in hospitals throughout the San Gabriel Valley for various ailments, all covered. Medicaire, Medi Cal, Medicaid, Medi everything. He was a valued customer. They would be sorry to see him give up the ghost.

Ian got fat-ass Dietrich out of the faculty lounge to cover him for the rest of the period, but only after assuring the lazy bastard all he had to do was babysit. Dietrich was the type that gave education a bad name, fodder for the anti-teacher element, of whom there was no shortage at Anesthesia. He could just hear them working themselves into a frenzy when their kids told them they had watched another movie. Wouldn't have been so bad if the films were even remotely relevant to what he was supposedly teaching, but what the hell had "Star Wars" to do with elementary algebra. How he was able to hold onto his job was anyone's guess, but he did, and never revealing any of the self doubt, that was so endemic to the profession. Without the protection of tenure, most would be basket cases. The problem was the arrangement protected bums like Dietrich.

Ah, well, Sloan noted as he watched the lump settle in behind his desk, one day he'll pop in the wrong tape – "Misty Serves the Home Team" instead of "Close Encounters of a Third Kind" and even tenure won't save him. Until then he'd take up space.

Martha arranged coverage for the rest of the day and Sloan instructed Julie to leave a note if there were any problems.

He felt very much the truant as he pulled out of the parking lot, yet glad, despite the circumstances, to escape. No need for the freeway; surface streets would get him there just as fast. He was not especially worried – he had been through this so many times before. As recently as last Christmas. Intensive care with pneumonia. The year before, kidney problems, six years earlier, the big one – a triple bypass. But time was running out; he knew it, but he wasn't sure the old man did. Emphysema and prostrate cancer, on top of everything else. A shuffling wreck. And leading the way, the oft broken bulbous nose with its multitude, of purple and scarlet Thomas Guide veins. He must have been a tough bastard when he was young, thought Ian. Deciding not to shoot the yellow, he rolled slowly up to the crosswalk.

He had heard all the stories, was nurtured on them, from the shipyards of Glasgow to the bars of Toronto and Detroit. Only 5'7" and hit like a heavyweight. As a child Ian had had witnessed the fury. A Sunday afternoon, the sidewalks crowded with post church strollers, men in suits and fedoras with wives and girlfriends in bright dresses and hats tamped down by the threat of the wind. A little boy waiting with his father for the light to change. The old man had been drinking, and even then, young as he was, Ian was sensitive to the condition. There had been harsh words at home, recriminations, and his mother had left, taking Petey with her.

The horn from the car behind brought him back and he accelerated. But where had they been going? After his mother and Petey? He could still remember his father moving in the stiff mannered gait of the drunk on display, pronounced, like the exaggerated steps of a dance instructor, placing one foot meticulously before the other, a concentrated strain that would soon ebb and abandon him altogether for a moment, leaving him to sway like a tree in a gust. And with much aplomb he would stop in the middle of the sidewalk to right himself. An abrupt halt, like the leader of a safari sensing danger, and he would finger his belt buckle, then reach up to his throat to caress the knot of his necktie and down to tug at the cuffs of his Sunday best shirt, meant only for Mass which he seldom attended. And the gold plated cufflinks from London, he was quick to point out whenever he wore them. The insignia crossed sabers…but where had they been going? He couldn't remember…no, his father wouldn't tell him, wouldn't say…but long minutes before

114

the mirror as dormant, heavy fingers struggled with the row of buttons and drew the necktie behind and across the throat and coming alive to form, a perfect Windsor knot; after all, it was Sunday…and the piece de resistance – the inserting of the crossed sabers.

The staring, the snickers, his father, head held high, seemingly oblivious, finding a new balance, set out again. Then something more direct than a stare or a laugh…something that could not be missed, a slight bump perhaps, then an exchange of words. A triviality. One of those inconsequential unpleasantries that liquor fomented to madness in a man like his father. The other, bigger, with a wide mouth, had stepped forward grinning, sleeves rolled, hands raised. He must have thought it all great fun to give the smaller fellow a good thumping.

And the old man, suddenly awakened, slipped into his crouch, sure-footed now, moved in, balanced, compact, head and shoulders dipping, shifting from side to side, the stalker, and the other now fixed, trying to set himself, wanting to strike, but not quite sure when. "C'mon, you son-of-a-bitch," his father sneered, ever nearer. The man's grin had vanished. A trace of apprehension, of fear even. But why? Only a drunk. A middle age stumbling drunk.

Taller and younger, he had meant it as a kind of game, an amusement on a boring Sunday, something to recount to his friends at work next day, but all had changed as he moved to throw a punch at his coiled opponent, but thought better of it. He was the traveler well onto the footbridge above the chasm who acknowledges too late his paralytic fear of heights.

He began inching backward before the crouching, taunting figure, who only moments before seemed on the verge of toppling. And puzzled by the sudden transformation, he sought to bring it all back to where it was, to resurrect the smile as he measured his opponent, as he steeled himself to strike at the bobbing head, but once again he faltered and that indecision, those crucial seconds, were his undoing.

The old man sprang, almost lifting himself from the sidewalk, fists a blur, no hesitation, never one to be concerned about consequences.

A perfect combination. The first blow stunned and in that moment when the man sought to pull his head out of range, the second came, crushing his nose, followed immediately by a thunderous right that caught him, nostrils dripping crimson, high on the temple, and the Sunday walker, the seeker of diversion, sagged, one arm reaching, as he collapsed forward, a ponderous, unchecked load, face down on the pavement, his arm, the left, the one that had betrayed him in its irresolution, lay crumpled beneath his chest, one of those distortions that calamity often brings. And a trickle of blood, unexpected from the unmarked ear, crept down the side of his face. He hadn't even thrown a punch.

And his father, when he saw the other make no attempt to rise, in fact had moved not at all, came closer, peering down, breathing heavily, clutching at Ian to keep his own self upright. Ian had started to cry and the crowd grew and pressed in and someone yelled, "Get an ambulance!" The rage gone, his father grabbed his shoulder and they hurried from the scene, never looking back.

The old man stayed home from work the next day, agitated, for a time pacing the kitchen, unable to sit with his coffee. Subdued conversations, whispered exchanges almost, as though the house were riddled with the listening devices so much a part of Cold War movies and television then.

His mother went out and his father lay down on the couch. She returned with two newspapers, though they only ever got the *Chronicle*, and spreading them across the kitchen table, pored over each.

By mid week, all was back to normal, normality as they knew it. His mother cautioned Ian never to speak of the incident.

# THIRTEEN

The room was semi private, the other bed unoccupied. His father, lord of the manor, lay ensconced in pillows staring up at the television. A woman with frizzled hair was narrating how she had escaped an abusive husband and lived three months in a self storage unit.

"Hello, Son."

"Hi, Dad."

"Sit down." He returned to the program. "Bloody pitiful…Did the doctor call you?"

"Yes."

"Sorry they bothered you at work…damnits, Ian, I took a fall." He looked gaunt, frail, but seemed in good spirits. A clear plastic tube was hooked up to his left arm.

"What happened?"

"I was going out. To the market across the street. Just a few things…necessities. When I got to the top of the stairs, I stepped down and just like that," he raised a trembling hand to his face, "I got all dizzy. Next bloody thing I know I'm lying at the foot of the stairs. Must have blacked out. Didn't feel a buggarin' thing. And there I am. Flat on my back. Look at this." He raised the arm with the tube.

"Be careful, it might come loose."

"Look at it," he demanded and held the slack, milky underside of the arm, stained a deep purple that ran to black. "Look at that bloody bruise...doctor said should have killed me, man my age. That's what he said, God's truth...the old man's plenty tough yet, huh, Son?"

"Did someone call an ambulance?"

"No ambulance...Pepe and his roommate. They took me to emergency in their car. Pepe heard the noise...a bloody racket, Ian. Pepe said it sounded like 'boom, boom.' He thought at first it was an earthquake. They carried me to the car and rushed me to the hospital. He's a good lad, Pepe. Mexican, but a nice kid ...my ribs is hurt too. I think I broke a couple...look." He pulled at the gown and grimaced. "I'm all wrapped up like a bloody package...not many as can take a fall like that."

"Don't disturb it." Ian reached to restrain him. "I'll look at it later."

"The buggarin' bandages is uncomfortable...terrible. You know, Son, I haven't broken my fast all day. Didn't have no breakfast. This bloody thing.." He stroked the tube. "They won't give me nothing solid."

"They will later. You have to be patient."

"Patient! Damnits! I'm starving. Some fish and chips would hit the spot."

"You can't have fish and chips in your condition."

"Buggar it! I feel fine."

"The doctor would never allow it."

"To hell with the doctor." They returned to the television and an obese man with long hair and a necklace who insisted that in a previous life he had been a woman, an American woman who ran a dance studio in Buenos Aires, thus explaining, he said, why he danced the tango so marvelously. "Disgusting," said his father but he did not change the channel.

The news came on and they fell into infrequent conversation. When the nurse arrived with his father's medicine, he took his leave, promising to return that evening.

The long, quiet, sterile hallway reinforced his aversion. Everything managed, controlled, distant. Outside Room 302 an older man with bulging gut in a red polo shirt was patting a woman's shoulder. She wept quietly and snuggled close to him. Ian slowed his pace as he approached the room. A nurse's aide moved briskly about the bed doing nothing where an elderly woman lay, eyes closed. Dry hands folded neatly across the chest proclaimed "enough."

At the nurses' station two Filipino aides talked and laughed, slipping in and out of English. One gave him a cursory glance. For all they knew, he might have just executed any number of the feeble; all he would need would be a pillow. Each room a death chamber. He could clear an entire ward in a half hour. Hospitals were not safe places.

As the elevator descended, he thought of growing old and dying in a white space, muffled sobbing at the door…but who would sob? Evelyn? Perhaps deciding it would be expected. Teddy? Probably not…a grown man…that was it then…end of journey.

Not for him. When he stepped out into the late afternoon sunlight, he told himself he would not die in such a place. None of the pity, none of the sadness, forced or otherwise, for him. He'd jump off the bridge first. By that time, though, he'd probably be too weak to pull himself over the railing.

He called Pete when he got home, but there was no answer. He left the directions and visiting hours on the answering machine but would wait to tell Evelyn until he had a better sense of his father's condition.

He found him in a wheelchair at the end of the hall, the tube dangling from a rack on wheels. His robe was drawn up around his throat, the few strands of hair, white wisps in various stages of verticality atop the parched scalp, like faltering sentries in some dry land. He was not wearing his glasses and his teeth were not in. An artist seeking to render defeat, might find no better subject:: One showing only, 'The Vanquished.'"

He assumed the old man was asleep, the head drooped in slumber. But as he drew near, Ian could see the eyes were open and for an instant he was stuck dumb, frozen…only he and the blank face…in that short distance, in that brief time.

He roused himself and crept closer. A slight rising and falling of the chest. He squatted next to the wheelchair, cowering almost, the way he crouched in the corner of the closet or under the bed when the old man awoke untimely from his Sunday nap and went searching, cursing under his breath, belt in hand, his mother pleading, *"He's only a child… just playing."*

"Dad." The head slowly raised, the eyes gazing blankly at him, lost, unable to focus, as though he had gone far away. Ian awaited his return.

"Hello, Son."

"What are you doing out here?"

"The…room. Couldn't stand it…I had to get out." The hall was busy. Staff attending to their duties, unconcerned. Just another of the enfeebled. In this place of care, no one seemed to care.

"You're not giving the nurses a bad time, are you? Serenading them?"

During his stay at San Gabriel Community he spoke with great pride of how much the nurses enjoyed his singing. He taught them, none of whom were even born when the song was popular, to harmonize on "Paper Doll." They assured him he had a wonderful voice, though in truth, little more than a whisper after a lifetime of cigarettes. Once there had been a voice, a lovely one. A young tough on the streets of Glasgow, yet soprano in the Port Glasgow Cathedral Choir. A beautiful voice when they first met, his mother said, pure, clear, "like a fine bird." He could reach notes others strained for, smoothly, effortlessly.

She knew she loved him that first night when he took her hand in his and sang, "I'll Take You Home Again, Kathleen."

"Push me to the window, Son." Ian guided the wheelchair and the rack over to the glass. His father leaned toward the window, trying to get beyond his own reflection, mesmerized by the headlights and tail-lights that fled him in the darkness below.

"That better?"

"I wish I was in one of those cars…going somewhere…anywhere."

"You will. You will…when you get out of here…we'll take a trip."

"Do you think we could, Son?" He gathered himself up, eyes intent. "A long trip?"

"Sure, a long trip."

"I want to go across the Golden Gate Bridge. It's a magnificent bridge, Son."

"Yes it is."

"Your Uncle John worked on it, you know. Dangerous bloody work. They put up a net to catch the ones that fell…I told you about your Uncle John."

"Yes, you did…we'll go across the bridge, and then across the country. We could visit the old house in Canada, if you want."

His thumb traced the vein that snaked down from just below the forearm. He pressed the skin and pulled it, like a sheet, back and forth, across the bones.

"It's hellish to get old…don't get old, Son."

"Everyone gets old…can't avoid it."

The old man sank back in the chair and stared at himself in the window.

# FOURTEEN

Ian Sloan's belief in God vacillated, but generally he came down on the affirmative. That was, however, the extent of his spiritual experience at present and mass that Sunday was his first since Teddy was a child. He slipped into a pew at the rear, knelt, blessed himself, sat back and waited. They had always settled in near the front. Teddy would have been four or five then and, fascinated by the Eucharist, wanted a clear view of the "little house" on the altar. Every Sunday he waited in anticipation of communion, convinced that tiny creatures dashed to and fro, busy preparing the white discs.

Evelyn was not Catholic and rarely accompanied them but had not objected to Teddy's being baptized or attending mass. But as Teddy grew older, they edged further and further back in the congregation. The ten a.m. service continued until the divorce. At first he had tried to keep the tradition alive but soon began to sense Evelyn's and Devon's displeasure, though neither had actually said anything. And Teddy's enthusiasm seemed to wane. He was growing up and Ian didn't want to apply any pressure, so by tacit agreement the ritual ceased.

He felt satisfied, though, that he had fulfilled his responsibility, despite never quite understanding what was expected in that regard. He supposed to give a spiritual anchor of sorts. At the very least expose him to the rite and let the boy chart his own course later. And really, what were the benefits? For himself a parochial education and Sunday mass had left little more than a handful of memories. In the end, what was there really, beyond the sentimental?

Just as the priest appeared, a family of three genuflected at his pew, and for a moment he could not decide whether to slide further down or stay put and make them squeeze by. He was reluctant to give up his position by the aisle, again, the unimpeded exit. Theaters, airplanes, churches, all the same – ease of departure. Something more for the therapists, but given the setting, he made the sacrifice and edged along the bench.

He retrieved the missal from the holder, determined to follow the liturgy. When he was a kid the service was in Latin, heavy lettered, archaic, and taxing of a boy's devotion. But accessibility came at a cost. With the shift to English, the veil had been lifted, the mystery removed, the clutter of antiquity cleared away, but so too was the grandeur, replaced by a spare pragmatism. Somehow, with the drama excised, the service lost its identity, like the newly reformed bon vivant, who having relinquished erstwhile vices and embraced sweat, a rooted diet, and a scheduled life, is no longer recognizable. Not simply the trimness, but the precision that followed, the rationed laugher, the lying down to uneventful slumber - all in the name of longevity.

The priest turned to bless the congregation and two guitarists, a young man and a young woman on folding chairs to the left of the altar, strummed softly. Soon their voices emerged, a mellifluous sound awakened, a choir of two that grew in intensity, their faces radiant. The celebrants responded and Sloan, absorbed in the priest and his accompaniment, forgot the missal and followed the others when they knelt and stood.

The sermon, something about the family as core of society, was less didactic than the discourses of his youth, delivered with less authority, more conversational, as if inviting commentary, as one who was indeed a friend of the family might speak.

But Ian was not really listening. His attention was drawn to the stained glass windows and the statues of Mary and Joseph, a relationship that had troubled him when he was young. The virgin birth. He had accepted it as a child, but adolescence brought a doubt that gnawed at him. Was Joseph not good enough? Not a theological question, rather a human one, the product of hormones, of sex, so much a part of those years, so consuming of boys at that age, always on the prowl, wishing only to drop their seed. A miracle, he knew, a matter of faith, but still it bothered him. Somehow Joseph was made inferior. Irrelevant. The perennial Prince Philip, a wooden nobody. Always the background piece. Could two such people be truly happy? Yet they had remained, Mary and Joseph, Elizabeth and Philip.

He continued, lost in the plaster robes, when he suddenly realized the sermon was over, the assemblage kneeling. He slid off the bench to his knees and took up his missal. He fumbled through the pages, somewhere between the gospel and the Eucharist, flipping back and forth, discreetly he hoped, when a small, delicate hand interrupted. The thumb and forefinger turned the pages three forward, the forefinger tracing down half way to the middle of the page. He nodded at the diminutive figure and smiled, and she of radiant brown eyes gave back in kind and returned to the mass.

An old-fashioned hair arrangement, long and straight, an awning of heavy bangs over the forehead. The prismatic light through the stained glass fell upon the glorious sheen, a beauty that would have been hidden beneath a kerchief in his more formal time, those days of Latin and authority.

Full, pinkish lips opening and closing in recitation. Unquestioned faith. For her, miracles. She bowed her head and her eyelashes fluttered as she struck her chest solemnly, once, twice, thrice. And when it came time for the greeting, another innovation he had difficulty accepting, she proffered her hand and said, "Peace be with you." He accepted the soft, warm touch, and a contentment came to him.

The host was elevated and the congregation knelt to pray their special intentions. Ian put his hands together and seeking to believe again prayed for his father, not that he would recover, but that he would die without suffering, physically or mentally. The old man had much to anguish over, but Ian did not want him to feel remorse. Such torment would serve no purpose. Regret was useless. And if indeed there was a last judgment, Ian prayed for leniency.

As the crowd filed out, he kept his eyes on the girl, her head and shoulders among the passing throng. In the vestibule he lost sight of her, and when he saw her again, the family was descending the steps in the opposite direction.

All the way home he could not get the little girl out of his mind. The unexpected joy, like turning a corner and stepping out of grayness into sunlight. One of those inexplicable moments that became a part of you, some more keenly felt than others, but all remaining to some degree.

Summer, nineteen, an L.A. novice with no car and a longing to experience the city, to know, he had boarded the bus at Pershing Square, returning from a production at the old Civic Light Opera, Alfred Drake in "Kismet." A theatergoer in suit and tie, he felt quite the sophisticate, a respite from the factory hours, Monday through Friday, standing before the presses waiting for the mold to open and offer its plastic trinket and five seconds to snip it free before the great iron jaws clamped tight again – 500 pieces a day.

The night was warm and she sat opposite holding a shopping bag in her lap, her back to the open window. The wind lifted her hair blowing it across her face. She laughed when she noticed him looking at her and in the back a kid with a portable radio turned up the volume on "Spanish

Harlem." The bus idled at a red light and the scent of night blooming jasmine swept into the coach. She swayed with the abrupt lunge and once again the hair draped itself over her lips. Flashes of white behind the lovely, dark mesh. A languid hand patiently removed the strands as if attending to an errant child. He wanted to speak to her, to draw back the filigree, to touch her cheek.

She pulled the cord and stepped forward tentatively, the bus rider's gait that undermines even the most graceful, yet her awkwardness had charm as she struggled up the aisle, one hand holding the bag, the other reaching out from pole to pole. He must say something, but what… what? Stay. He wanted to tell her to stay, but he did not, could not, and so he remained, mute, as the doors opened and she stepped down into the night. He sprang to her seat. Passengers were boarding. There was still time to…to call to her…to tell her, "Don't go! Please…don't go." before she vanished.

Perhaps if they had had a girl.

# FIFTEEN

Hers was the third on the right, eight in total that rose modestly on a worn, grassy knoll bisected by a concrete walkway terminating at the base of a towering palm. In the darkness, homey cottages, a welcoming glow from behind drawn curtains. Indeed, seen at night, even a Vivian Shelby, for whom "cottage" evoked a thatched roof, baby roses wending above an oaken door, hinged, secure against all weathers and fronting and enchanting patch of garden, might succumb to the illusion. And within by fireside the devoted one waiting, kettle on, Browning in hand. Yes, Vivian could embrace such an image.

In truth, hopeless dens on gray, forlorn days, confining, sweltering hot boxes on interminable summer afternoons, the ubiquitous freeway drone in the distance and...Grace the checker.

He paused at the door. The black metal 3 that hung upside down and backwards metamorphosed into a half eight. Next to the concrete landing, more pedestal than porch, barely surface enough for two abreast, a pink and gold scooter lay abandoned on its side in the dirt. Apparently Ben was not much for parking.

He was riveted by the puncture in the door where the top of the three should have been and was about to knock when epiphany-like he saw himself, a middle-age man holding a paper bag, hovering above

Ben's transportation. What the hell was he doing here? But there was no number. She had read him well. Unable to call, they both knew he lacked the courage not to show up. Anyway, he rationalized, if he didn't, he'd have to find somewhere else to shop, and if anything he was a man of routine. There had to be some certainties in life.

"What are you standing there for? C'mon in." She grinned and stepped back. "You should've knocked, the doorbell don't work. Ben saw you coming up the walk. He likes to peek through the curtains… check out what's going on…big snoop."

Ben was lying on his stomach before the television in Superman pajamas, thumb in his mouth, staring at a "Star Trek" rerun.

"Hi, Ben."

"Ben 's a 'Trekkie,' aren't you, Big Fella?"

The boy spun around, legs spread-eagle in interplanetary salute. A reddish, yellow stain stretched from just below the S down to the waist. Superman had already dined.

"Have a seat."

"I brought some beer." He handed her the bag. "I don't know what kind of wine goes with Mexican food."

"Me neither…oh, wow! Lowenbrau. Nothin' but the best for us. Still cold…sit down, sit down…relax. I got some chips and salsa ready."

She disappeared into a kitchen that, from where he sat, looked even smaller than his own. One of those cramped spaces that attract when one is young and of romantic disposition, that interlude before income, debt, and ambition take hold and tiny rooms became merely depressing. At his father's age, funereal.

In his pre-Evelyn days he had a second-floor one-bedroom with French windows and a small balcony with a deep green iron railing, the perch more decorative than useful. Whenever he opened the windows wide to the canopy of pepper trees opposite, he imagined grand boulevards. The Champs Elysees. Paris, City of Light. Chestnut trees. Sprawling cafes. Pretty women sipping aperitifs.

"Try this. I made it myself, from scratch." She placed a bowl of fresh salsa and chips and a bottle of beer on the coffee table. "You want a glass?" She remained standing in denim overalls and a pink t-shirt with blue lettering that read "Cash and Carry" across her breasts, the straps strategically concealing her braless nipples.

"Yes, please."

"Ian, you're so polite. God, I just love that…guys now, you know, so immature and no manners…Ben, say 'scuse me.'" Ben excused himself and farted again. "Ben!"

"Scuse me." Despite the contrition, Ian knew he hadn't heard the last from Superman.

The meager living room was dominated by a 30" television. Grace was eclectic in her furnishings. A large poster was festooned to each of the three walls: a brooding, trench-coated James Dean in rainy Times Square faced off with a tomato red Mercedes, while a pouting, deep cleavaged Marilyn Monroe played intermediary from the north wall. Above the couch where he sat, an empty canvas awaited the decorator's hand. A corner table held an electric glass sculpture he couldn't quite grasp. A score of thin cylinders, each a slender, incandescent light that shot up from a black base. Either a bouquet or a nuclear explosion.

"There's Skelter, Ben." She pointed her beer at a ginger cat creeping out from under the couch.

"Skeller! Skeller!" Superman crawled toward the cat, which had stopped to clean itself.

"Helter! Helter!" called Grace. "Come out and meet our guest." In due course, black fur with yellow eyes, emerged slowly, hesitantly, head jerking from side to side, from behind the television. Ben turned to the new arrival.

"Ever read *Helter Skelter*?" said Grace.

"No, never did."

"Man, old Charlie Manson...weird dude. I don't remember much of it...I was just a little kid. But I read *Helter Skelter* and I saw him on tv. One of those true life programs on killers...he's creepy."

"That he is."

"Those girls worshipped him. Man, he could get them to do anything." She gulped some beer and repeated with emphasis: "I mean anything...Was everybody all nervous and scared with him out there roaming around?"

"I think a lot were...for a while, anyway."

"I would have been, I can tell you that. They all lived on an old ranch way out in the Valley...Dopin' all the time...orgies. His girls would do anything for him...You think he pimped them?"

"I don't know."

"Was the trial on tv?"

"No. Lots of coverage but no cameras in the courtroom."

"Wow! That must have been something...Remember Son of Sam? Another crazy shit."

"Oh, yeah."

"I remember I was a freshman when school started that year... you know, I was scared to sit with a guy in a car. I just couldn't relax. I was always thinking someone was watching and he'd sneak up when we were gettin' it on...I just couldn't relax, you know what I mean?"

"I think so."

"So many weirdoes. Wonder what makes them do it?" She reached for a chip and then held it, lost in thought, but Sloan felt he comprehended a little of their madness. Would this be the topic of the evening? A Who's Who of Homicidal Maniacs. America's Top Ten. Best by Category: Most Adept with a Razor; Most Proficient with a Hammer.

"Elway, Mommy. Elway."

"Ben wants to show you his rabbit…out back." She pointed to the kitchen.

Superman led the way out the rear door to where a spotted rabbit crouched in the darkness nibbling pellets and sniffing the night air from behind a circle of chicken wire that enclosed a narrow plot of dirt and weeds. Ben circled the perimeter calling to the creature, but his endearments went unheeded.

"Time to eat…go ahead Ian. I'm gonna put Ben to bed…let's go Superman. Bedtime for you, buddy."

The boy followed his mother to the bedroom, where he lingered in the door-way, tugging on her overalls. When Grace crouched to him, he put his hand to his mouth and whispered, all the while casting furtive glances toward the kitchen. "Ben wants to give you a hug."

Superman dashed across the room and Ian, girding for the onslaught, raised his arm. "That's okay, he doesn't have to." Ben drew up short, confused.

"No, siree," said Grace. "Ben don't hug just anybody. But when he decides to hug, that's it. You don't say 'no.' to Ben."

"Like his mother." She laughed and Ben completed the assault.

She was as good as her word. The tamale pie was thick and delicious. She talked and ate; he ate and nodded. He still wished he hadn't come but decided he might as well make the best of it. Three beers went down easily, leaving him lightheaded by meal's end.

"I'm stuffed," said Grace. "That was good, even if I do say so myself."

"Really good. You're a great cook."

"Well, thank you, sir…I told you I was, didn't I? You gotta believe a girl when she tells you she's good at something." She grinned, lowering the straps of the overalls and pulling up the t-shirt up and out from her waist, exposing a milky stretch of midriff. "God I'm full." She stood to clear the table and her nipples, clearly defined beneath the cotton shirt, beckoned. He hurried to gather up the bottles.

"Save the caps. I keep them for Ben; he loves the Broncos. That's why he named his rabbit Elway. He thinks he's John Elway. Throws them all over the place whenever the Broncos are on. He's always losing them. That's one thing about those foreign beers. You have to use an opener and it bends the caps… you go in and sit down. I'll just be a few minutes."

"I'll help you."

"No, that's okay…see what's on tv. I'll be right in. I'll just rinse them off."

He knew what was coming and wasn't sure how he'd respond. Her body, generous though it was and celibate though he had been for more than two years, held little appeal. He could hear her stacking the dishes and was tempted to slip quietly out the front door…no ridiculous. Even he wasn't that heartless. Besides, he wasn't sure he had the strength to get up. All he really wanted was to stretch out on the couch.

"Anything on?" She flopped down next to him and grabbed the remote. "Hey, look, 'Rambo, First Blood.' Ever see it?"

"No…No, haven't had the pleasure." Her easy familiarity, her manner, her speech, her dress – her ponderousness overwhelmed him, made him uncomfortable, irritated, and once again, despite the food, he wished he had not come..

"He's so buff. Look at him, he's…"

"A fool."

Grace was stunned. "Did you ever see 'Rocky'? The first 'Rocky'?"

"No, I have been spared."

"You missed a good movie. So emotional. So inspiring…and you learn a lot about boxing."

"Fairy tale. Soap opera. If you want to see a good fight movie, rent 'Fat City.'"

"Never heard of it."

"Most people haven't...realistic, none of that phony crap. Good characterization. Good dialogue..."

"Lighten up." She leaned close to him. "You know what?"

"What?"

"I think you're just jealous."

"Yeah...I am."

"He's a stud and he's getting' up there. He's over forty. Look at that body."

"But his brain has remained young... very young."

"I don't care what you say. Sly Stallone's a hunk and "Rocky's" a great movie. You're just too negative."

"You're right."

"I was watching a talk show and this psychiatrist...psychologist. Whatever he was. He said that thinking negative thoughts all the time will make you get old faster."

"Is that right?"

"Yes, that's right, Mister. You should have seen him. He was 51 but he looked like he was in his thirties."

"Really?"

"I know you don't believe me but..."

"No, no...if it's on television, it must be true...By the way, is there going to be another Rocky? We've only had what, three, four?"

"Are you making fun of me?" She pulled away, mouth open as if she were sucking air from a Rocky hook to the kidneys, and Sloan realized what a jerk he was. She had invited him into her home, fed him, tried to make him comfortable. And in return, was belittled by an arrogant, condescending bastard.

"No, I'm sorry. Just trying to be funny. I'm sorry." He placed his hand on her knee and she bounced up from the couch.

"I've got something you'll like."

"What…what's that?" Christ! Was the shirt coming off?

"Tequila! Girl at work brought me a bottle from TJ. I haven't opened it yet."

"I don't think I've ever had tequila."

"You don't know what you're missing." He could hear the cupboards opening and closing. What the hell, a long time since he had been drunk.

"I got a video you'll like too." She set the bottle, two shot glasses, lime wedges and a salt shaker on the table.

"Shit!…Sophie borrowed it…no…I don't think so…" She stretched forward on her haunches, her big farmer's ass taunting him as she rummaged through the cabinet below the television. "Look in the drawer, will you?" She pointed to the end table.

"I found it…you weren't supposed to see that." She took the dildo and dropped it into the cavanerous overalls pocket. "Not as good as the real thing, but…when you're horny, you're horny." She pushed in the cartridge.

The tape had only been partially rewound. No cast credit here. The screen filled with a blond giving head to a Rocky type sitting on the edge of a pool. She was standing topless, half out of the water. Probably shot in the Valley, yet there seemed to be altitude. Maybe the Hollywood Hills. Didn't matter where, pornography ultimately depressed him. After the initial titillation, in the end it left him depressed.

"Dumb shit. Why would you rewind only half way."

"Maybe Sophie got interrupted," he said, "but I think we can pick up the story line."

Grace insisted on rewinding completely so they could start with Mario's arrival to clean the pool.

"A linear narrative," said Sloan. He couldn't help himself, but Grace was not listening. She was engrossed in Mario, who had slipped into the kitchen next door to display his prowess to an unconvincingly startled housewife, blondie's neighbor, who by chance was wearing nothing but an apron and rubber gloves. How often he thought must she have stared at those images alone in that cramped room. Yet still it excited and soon she was rubbing him too.

"You're so soft." She pulled the t-shirt up over her head. Her arms extended, he started nuzzling her pride, those great mother tits. She giggled and cooed and led him, straps dangling, into the darkened bedroom and hurried out of her overalls. She wore no underwear and stood waiting, a great bonanza of flesh as he struggled with his shirt. Superman turned in his sleep and sighed.

"What about Ben?" he whispered.

"Ben's fine." With deft hands she undid his belt, loosened the button, and unzipped his pants. And in those uncertain shadows, his separate, weightless self submitted.

"He might wake up." She removed his shirt, turning him one way then the other as she pulled down each sleeve, guiding him as if he were a Ben himself now.

"I'll move him to the couch." She approached the curled body in all her white nakedness.

"No! Don't touch him."

She froze, and in that murky light a flicker of anxiety, fear even, all her assumptions undermined, no longer certain who it was she was bedding…a Charlie Manson…Son of Sam… Murderer, serial killer, latent for years, burrowed deep in his ordinariness, now sprung to life. A simple schoolteacher, middle age, weary, a sarcastic bastard, biding time in his blood lust.

And to Sloan her silence, her absolute stillness, was a growing recognition of the familiar, a plain of disregard, rebuff, rejection, disappointment, all tomorrows an ever narrowing repetition, yet always the longing for another. For one who remained…for love.

"What's wrong?"

137

"Nothing...I...let's not disturb him. You're right. He probably won't wake up."

He lay still listening to the clock on the nightstand. She had tried to reassure him, console him, told him not to worry, not to feel bad. Those things happened. It was okay with her. He wanted to tell her he wasn't bothered in the least. In fact, he was relieved. But he let her ramble on until at last she joined Ben in dreamland.

For what seemed an interminable time, he remained motionless, her arm flung across his chest, staring at the ceiling. In youth the same, in the stillness, thinking...listening.

*"He has to learn sometime."*

*"Don't talk bloody nonsense."*

*"It's not nonsense. His body's changing and better now,"* she insisted, *"so he won't have problems later...worrying about it. So he can understand properly."*

*"Bloody nonsense,"* a cough and then another until the spasm reached a crescendo. He had been raised on the hacking, could see how the shoulders would sway and how he would remove the glasses, his eyes watery, the deep wheezing breaths, *"Jesus-boy-oh-boy."* And when the chest had settled, he would reach for the pack, Players Fine Cut or Philip Morris, and light up.

*"If you don't talk to him, I will."*

*"Bugger it! Say nothing...you'll only confuse the boy."* The chair scraped and he saw him in his undershirt leaning against the sink, inhaling deeply, adamant. Another cigarette and he prevailed.

But no longer. Time was running out. He wouldn't last more than a few weeks, at most; his doctor had said as much...Teddy had assured him no drugs. But there were other ways to be sick, to be addicted... Evelyn was, in her own way...Pete hadn't even called. But Ian knew damn well when the old man died, his brother would arrange an elaborate service, give the eulogy…he'd be goddamned if he would attend.

Grace lay, head against his shoulder, mouth agape, breathing strongly. And from Ben in the corner, the occasional murmur. And he knew Superman would never fly.

He rolled over and her arm followed. The bedding smelled of vanilla and the itch began behind his knee, then his calf and ankle.

He rubbed the other foot, the one with the jagged nail on the big toe, up and down his calf. Finally, he could stand it no longer and slipped out from under the sheet. Her arm followed and she mumbled something about breakfast but did not awaken.

He had the pants and shirt on but could not locate his shoes. He was on his hands and knees, groping under the bed until he remembered he had taken them off in the living room. When he got to his feet, Ben was sitting up sucking his thumb and staring at him. Ian put his fingers to his lips: "Shh." Ben farted and giggled.


The night was damp and foggy and his head was killing him. Someone had tossed a pizza carton, one piece splattered, topping down, on the hood of the Rabbit.

All the way home a string of self recriminations. She'd get over it, he told himself. Grace was resilient. He had to give her marks for that. She required little – full stomach, something to watch on her 30" screen, the occasional fuck. She wanted more, but would take less… whatever was available.

The fog thickened and the wipers were of little help. The high beams

only made it worse. He slowed to a crawl and still almost missed his turn. His front tires were already in the crosswalk when he saw her, pushing a loaded grocery cart. He brushed the front of the cart and she raised her arm as if to ward him off. She shook her finger and cursed when he rolled down the window to apologize. He was about to get out to make sure she was okay but she was becoming more and more incoherent so he drove off, his heart still racing

He turned off the engine but remained sitting in the carport, cold and shaking, his head still throbbing. The fog had settled, an enveloping gray and he could only just make out the stairway at the rear of the building.

He shivered and fumbled for a cigarette. The flame quivered and he had to concentrate to light up. He felt exhausted, disinterested, inert. Was this what Victorian writers referred to as malaise, ennui? The affliction of those Jamesian aristocrats who, having grown weary, with nothing more to stimulate, the scones having been nibbled, the tea having cooled, slipped into oblivion, expiring finally, in a lawn chair on a summer afternoon on an estate in Kent, or some such place. Or the cynical, jaded hero, having dissipated his passion, attaches himself on a whim to a cause, which he may or may not believe in, and in dramatic fashion discards what is left.

No, he was neither. He had not done enough or seen enough to be bored with living and he would never have the courage for martyrdom, intended or otherwise. The simple depression that came with age, a sense of hopelessness. But why? He was financially stable and, as far as he knew, in good health. A respectable, secure job. He would never get rich, but money had never been terribly important to him. At the very least he should be grateful for not having run over that poor son-of-a-bitch. And he was…yet, he felt so goddamned unhappy. So sad he wanted to cry.

His stiffened arms pressed down on the steering wheel. "Jesus Christ!" He slumped forward, his head on his forearm. He told himself if he had any guts he'd drive to the bridge right now and jump…into the void. Instead, he dragged himself up to bed.

# SIXTEEN

He stood watching for a moment before entering the room. Two additional tubes, long, thin, clear lines, that crept like tendrils from beneath the sheets and trailed from view on the other side of the bed. The urologist, an arid looking fellow of indeterminate age and bad posture who seemed himself to need a good pee, told him the most pressing concern was the kidneys. The old man had not urinated in two days the accumulated uremic acid reaching dangerous levels – the organs were simply shutting down, the first of the lights to be extinguished at that decrepit address.

His father had clearly deteriorated, a smaller presence, as though having withdrawn into the white gown, overwhelmed by the bedding and the vast pillows. Was this the person who had once terrified him so? As if reading his mind, the old man turned a pleading, winter face to him. Emerging from the depths a withered hand motioned Ian to come near.

"How are you feeling, Dad?" He couldn't quite catch the reply and pulled his chair closer.

"Bad night, Son. Very bad night." His eyes liquid, appealing. As a boy the exposed face, the heavy-framed, thick lenses removed, petrified him; awakened and stumbling without them he was for Ian a horror.

A squinting, monstrous hardness, an implacability that could not be breached, an anger that would, that must be vented. But now, the features having melded together, all ferocity had faded into uncertainty, vulnerability... fear.

"Were you in pain?...I can't hear you." He tilted his ear close to his father's mouth.

"Damnits, it was terrible," he moaned. "Terrible bloody pain...I can't piss, Son." The crudeness stunned him. His father had always said "pee." Why the change? Was he in his condition forgetting, returning to a coarseness, to the language of the street,,, to his real self?

"Did the doctor give you anything for the pain?"

"They don't care...let me have some water...mouth's so dry." He held the glass to his father's lips, grainy white, as if someone had sprinkled salt on them while he slept. He raised his head to swallow and covered Ian's hand with his own, his fingers bony and cold. The Adams apple bobbed twice. "That's better." The voice grew stronger. "Last night I wanted to die. I thought about suicide. Pull these bloody things out...but...I know it's a sin."

"Don't talk like that. You'll be better soon."

"You don't know what I been through, Son. Absolute agony. Absolute, bloody agony."

"I know but..."

"No, you bloody don't." He tried to raise his head, his breathing quickened. "You don't know..."

"Okay. Okay. Relax...You can't get excited. It's not good for you." The old man closed his eyes and took a few deep breaths.

"How are you, Lad?" he said, after a long silence. His father hadn't used the endearment in many years, but then "lads" were forever young. "Have you been eatin' regular?"

"Yes...yes, fine."

"I can't eat nothin'…look at the card Pety sent. Beautiful card." He started to reach toward the table on the other side of the bed but was too weak and settled for pointing.

A blue pond with geese flying among the clouds overhead and inside, "Get well soon, Love, Pete and Britt." Not his brother's handwriting.

"Lovely card, isn't it?"

"Yes, very nice."

"Pety's a good boy. He's doing good too…you never had an interest in business."

"No, I didn't."

"Do you see each other much?"

"Not much; we're both busy, I guess."

"You're not so busy you can't visit your little brother…have to watch out for him, Ian."

"Pete's fine. He's doing well."

"Good…let me have some more water, Son." He drew on the straw, paused to catch his breath, and drank some more. "Funny how Pety turned out so successful… ambitious boy, Pety. Always was."

"Yes."

"Ah, well, everybody's different…Son, I want you to do something for me."

"What's that?"

"You have the key to my room, don't you?"

"You told them to give it to me."

"Good. Good. Now listen…I want you to go to my room…and be careful. So many nosy bastards there. You can't trust none of them. You know the radio by my bed?"

"Yes, I know."

"In the back of it…" The coughing seized without warning, a rattle that quickly reached its apex, leaving him gasping. Ian thought of Beatrice at school, soulmates, the two of them, veterans of the nicotine wars, back to the days when a cigarette was really a smoke. No filters for them. He waited for his father to catch his breath then raised the glass to his mouth.

"Thanks, Son. Damnits. It hurts when I cough…don't smoke, Ian…where was I?"

"The radio in your room."

"Ah…in the back there's a covering, just a plastic thing held by four screws. You don't need a screwdriver. A knife will do." He stopped for a deep breath. "There's a knife and fork in the drawer." He paused again, waiting for Ian's reaction.

"I know where it is."

"All right…take the knife and unscrew the covering. There's a roll of bills, twelve hundred, maybe thirteen. I just forget now. A rubber band around them…unplug the radio. You don't want to electrocute yourself."

"Where did you get so much money?"

"Sh! Sh!" The trembling finger touched his mouth as he glanced at the curtain that separated him from the still empty bed. "Keep your voice down."

"Nobody can hear us."

"Well…I was having a good run at Santa Anita before I took that bloody fall. I can only keep a certain amount in the bank, you know. If you have too much, the welfare people they'll cut you off. They're very strict."

"I see."

"I want you to take enough for my rent, $285, and pay the manager. It's due the first of the month. I don't want her to get somebody else in there while I'm away…just like them to do that, you know…then they can raise the rent, the guttersnipes." Ian gazed at his father and the old man stared back, then dropped his eyes and tugged at the sheet, pulling it up to his throat and lifting his shoulder like a receiver bracing for a hit. "What's the matter?"

"Nothing…Nothing. Do you want me to bring you the rest of the money?"

"No, damnits! No! I don't want the bloody hospital to know. You hold on to it…I'll get it later. And, Ian, be quiet about it. Keep the door closed. You can't trust nobody. They're a nasty bunch of buggers. Except Pepe. I want you to give Pepe something for helping me…you know, to show my appreciation."

"I will."

"Thanks, Son…see what's on tv." Ian flipped the channels, lingering over whatever caught the old man's interest. They settled on a Lawrence Welk rerun. The Lennon Sisters were singing the old songs and his father kept time with his fingers on the sheet, a medley of Mills Brothers hits.

"Remember, Lad? We used to sing them all…You had a good voice…not as good as your old man's but…"

"I remember." He would place Pety and him on either side of the kitchen table on those Saturday nights when he stayed home, when he wasn't drinking, and lead them through "Up the Lazy River," "Glowworm," "Paper Doll" and his other favorites, "Too Young" and "Galway Bay." He tried to teach them harmony but they were hopeless and when they missed badly in their eagerness to please, he would laugh and shake his head. A mocking, derisive laugh. He watched his father trying to get the words out:

"I'm going to buy myself a paper doll…" he struggled, the lyrics reduced to tissue utterances.

"Oh, damnits, I don't have the strength."

"Take it easy. Don't overdo it." He offered more water, but his father waved it off. "I better get going. Visiting hours are almost over."

"It's good to see you, Son."

"Dad?"

"Yes, Son."

"I was wondering…I was just thinking…would you like to see a priest?"

"A priest?" he repeated, his voice rising.

"I just thought…probably been a while."The old man hesitated, his eyes wary, searching the room before returning to Ian.

"If you think…maybe I should."

# SEVENTEEN

"Armed guards! My God, this is Anesthesia High School," said John Collins, his bald pate glistening as he wrestled with the macaroni and cheese he had left too long in the microwave.

"John, face it. The town's changed," said Roth, but for Collins, who had never taught anywhere else, the essential Anesthesia was fixed, constant as the night sky. He loved the school, the community. This was home, though not literally. He could never have afforded to live in Anesthesia.

"Yes, it's changed…but only on the surface. Change is inevitable, but Anesthesia kids are basically the same as they've ever been. We've never had the problems,,, at least not as many…not as severe as other districts. Anesthesia is unique, right Vivian?"

Vivian looked up from her brie and water crackers and the apple she was sectioning to grant an exquisite smile. She spoke little. All would agree her presence was enough. They understood she was saving herself for the classroom. Oh, she might offer the occasional comment on a play she had attended or a novel recently read, usually British. She felt drawn to British authors, to their "luminous prose." Yes, her simply gracing their table was enough, anything more sheer largess. And all but Roth were duly grateful. He found her annoying. She and Collins were the longest tenured, though she a decade more, and both felt proprietary of the school and the town. But there the similarities ended. He of social studies and a Cal State education was more tolerated than embraced, and his attire: jeans and plaid shirts, decidedly common.

"We know we've got problems. Alf's been patrolling the campus two years now," added Roth.

"But Alf's not a police officer," said Collins. "He's not in uniform. The Board's proposing to put an officer in uniform with a weapon on campus every day. I see this as an obstacle to education and to the mutual trust and respect we've built up with our students over the years." Collins took great pride in being accessible, viewing his students more as companions than charges. He was one on whom they could depend. And like the departed Sammy, an easy A.

"John, we've had what, three, four drug busts on campus this year and we've still got three months to go." He didn't know about the others, but he saw the irony. The staff radical, the lefty, liberal, the neo hippy, defending the establishment, but he understood the value of intimidation, the importance of consequences. Naivete was fatal.

"I realize that, but there are better ways of solving the problem. Anyway, I heard they were inter district transfers. They're not our kids."

"Only one is interdistrict," said Roth. "At least two are good old, home-grown Anesthesiaites, born and bred."

Collins's was not the complete innocence of the late Senile Sammy, though; he knew there were some offenders. He simply believed any kid could be reasoned with, shown the error of his ways. Strike the right chord and every one was salvageable. He wished he were in a position to illustrate more officially. That was his one regret at not becoming a counselor. Of course, informally he did counsel, but it was not quite the same. He had once considered returning to school at night and taking the required courses, but never quite got around to it. Yet he remained convinced he would have been a natural.

"None of this would be necessary," observed Olivia Turnbull, "if the Board budgeted more for curriculum development. Look how they slashed Fine Arts at this school: Edwin's AP art class is gone; Sharon is down to one choral section; and I just found out they're cutting one of my drama classes next year. It's ridiculous!" She inhaled deeply and adjusted the silk scarf around her throat.

Olivia was very much attached to scarves. She had learned too late that one must have style, uniqueness…a presence – sadly, talent alone was not enough. The theater demanded more, much more. Had she realized that, among other things, when she was young, she might never have left New York. No question about talent. Everyone told her so, and she had been so hopeful. That was all gone now, but at least she could pass on the hard-earned knowledge to her thespians in waiting, a third of whom dropped at mid semester when they realized the stage was more than dressing up: memorization was hard work.

In addition to showing a flair for style, captured for the ages in the yearbook, her annual playbill, in which she was pleased to note her mug shot consistently the smartest, Olivia's scarves served another, more practical and ultimately more significant purpose: concealment.

Subterranean forces had been stealthily tugging, dismantling in tiny increments, generating a collapse she was powerless to check. At night in the sanctum of here boudoir she pored over the inexorable descent, studied her throat from different angles with hand mirrors, large and small, at times simultaneously. Various poses, which the most flattering, which to be avoided. That once smooth, slender, elegant part of her remained all but hidden now, a recluse to vanity. To recapture that lost beauty, she spent extravagantly on creams, lotions, imported soaps from France, Belgium, Italy, and experimented with unconventional treatments, once sleeping for several weeks with a soft rubber ball tucked under her chin. All to no avail. But Olivia was not unrealistic; she had come to accept that she could not undo nature. She would be content with a holding action of sorts, but even that was not to be. The subtle deterioration was relentless. Not yet fifty, she already had the elderly woman's chicken neck and many a night, recalling the swan that was, she cried herself to sleep.

A widow, she had lost her husband prematurely, thirty eight. A Saturday morning in summer. A fervent Dodgers fan, he looked forward to reading the game summary and studying the box score. She watched him from the kitchen going down the driveway. She reached for a cup and by the time she turned back, there he lay, face down on the concrete, a brain aneurysm. Her only solace Fletcher's not bearing witness to his leading lady's decline. He only knew her, loved her, before the fall, and in that she took comfort.

Olivia Turnbull was a trouper, though, and each morning, without fail, before the curtain rose, she would select a scarf, place it just so, fasten the pin, then step forward to embrace the footlights for yet another performance.

"Good point, Olivia." Collins warmed to his ally.

"Many recent studies have shown the value of the arts in a child's development," Olivia continued. "Psychologically, emotionally, very beneficial. Stimulates creativity and harmony. Eliminates tension, builds self esteem."

"Olivia's right."

"Ian, what's your take on it?" Roth called to Sloan, who had just found a note from Bengstrom in his box requesting a meeting during his free period to discuss "an important matter."

"What's that?"

"Having an armed security guard on campus."

"All for it....and guard dogs, Dobermen,,, and razor wire."

"I rest my case."

# EIGHTEEN

"Sit down, Sloan." Bengstrom appeared to be reading intently, but Ian didn't quite buy it. With the principal everything was calculated, done for effect. Comedy, tragedy, all the same. The point was to affect. And "The Great Dane" could be effectively serious, sad, gregarious – a man for all occasions, in all seasons. When his career in education was over, a second awaited: "Rent-a-Bengstrom." Weddings, funerals, bar mitzvahs, birthdays, store openings, reopenings – endless possibilities, thought Ian.

Sloan had immediately noted the latest addition. A Special Olympics poster above the bookcase just behind the principal's desk. Two children struggling to the finish line, ecstatic smiles on the flat, putty faces, and below in foot high dot matrix lettering, a banner he probably had Anthony in computers make up: HEART IS EVERYTHING.

"The Great Dane" jotted a few words and replaced the top of the fountain pen – he preferred ink to ballpoint, even for routine correspondence, because it was more precise and "The precision of the instrument enhances the precision of the writing."

"I'll come right to the point, Sloan. I'm not happy." Join the club, thought Ian.

"What's the problem?"

"The same 'problem' as before – the *Roar*."

"I don't understand."

"Let me ask you: What is the purpose of a student publication?" The fluorescent light directly above illuminated the strain, the shadows, like tire tracks down the sunken cheeks. No word yet on a new contract.

"I suppose to report…"

"In my time in education, it has always been my belief, and I dare-say just about every teacher and administrator in this district would agree with me, that the purpose of a student publication is to enrich the quality of school life." He stopped, allowing Ian to absorb the implications. "I overlooked Roth's letter in the last issue. He has a right to his opinion, but I can tell you, Mrs. Sobel was very angry and hurt. Believe me, we heard from her." Ian knew the "we" really meant "I." "Some have even suggested it smacked of anti-Semitism. I'm not prepared to go that far, but is it really a label we want associated with Anesthesia?"

"That's ridiculous. Anyone who knows Roth knows that's absurd. In fact, he's Jewish himself."

"I know that. The point is the letter created unpleasantness and misunderstanding."

"He wasn't trying to offend Mrs. Sobel. He just resents her inter-ference. He doesn't want her dictating how he uses class time. Any teacher would feel the same."

"Point taken. But now we have the Fanning girl stirring up more trouble. She was in here this morning wanting to know what I knew about the company that services the swimming pool. She said she was giving me the courtesy of speaking with her before she goes to the District Office. 'The courtesy!' What's wrong with that girl? Who does she think she is?"

Julie had come to him last week all excited and indignant, her vein a purple wrath. One of her friends had overheard her mother telling someone that apparently Assistant Superintendent Ed Vincent's nephew was given the contract without having to bid on it.

"Nothing wrong with her. She's an excellent editor and a fine writer. She's just gathering information, that's all."

"But why? Who cares about a swimming pool contract? My God, there are so many interesting subjects to write about."

"At the moment, I'm not sure what she's going to write, if anything. I guess it pretty much depends on what she learns."

"You better have a talk with her. Straighten her out." His hulk followed his jutting chin out over the desk and Sloan remained silent. He never looked for trouble and now that he was solidly middle age it was certainly not on his agenda. He hadn't always been that way. The old man had drilled into him never to take shit from anyone.. The dictum was so entrenched, so consuming, that in youth he could not ignore even the mildest affront. Better to get your ass kicked than kiss someone else's. Bloody noses, cut lips, bruises, integral parts, all, of his childhood. Adolescence brought some control. And there was an outlet. The all boys parochial school he attended offered boxing as a midwinter alternative to basketball and Ian took naturally to the sport. Four years, a champion in two weight divisions, 15-2 record, all to please the old man, his tutor and he had been an apt student.

While his peers watched television before bed, tired from the after school training and the evening's homework, he followed his father down into the basement. The calisthenics to warm up, then the drills, the same routine, night after night. Like a dancer, slow dancing in the center of the imaginary ring. Let the feet glide, balanced, no bouncing. Two steps forward, one back, one to the side, hands held high. Step into the jab, but snap it, ramrod stiff, striking at the end of the extension, *"most valuable bloody punch, Lad. Sets everything up,"* followed immediately by a straight right. The opponent's forward movement doubled the impact. A simple formula. The British school, slicing, centered blows. Defense was anticipation, minimal movement, maximum effect. One step back, two at most, just out of range, still close for the quick counterpunch. Straight, piston combinations. Make them pay, make them so tentative they fought not to get hurt.

He was well into his twenties before he was able to harness the pride, escape the paranoia of the imagined insult, yet even at this late date, it sometimes surfaced.

"I don't want to force her to bring everything to me for approval. I don't think..."

"You can't."

"Pardon?"

"You can't censor a school newspaper. It's been tried. The courts have upheld the freedom of the press for school newspapers. They have the same rights as any other publication."

"You're supposed to be providing guidance for these kids. You're their mentor. They take their lead from you." He sprang to his feet and stepped quickly from behind the desk. Ian thought for a moment they might actually duke it out, right there, among the quotes and the photos and the tributes. Sloan was already measuring the distance to the Bengstrom's gut, a right hook, solid, dip your shoulder, bring the weight behind, but snap it.

"The Great Dane" did not attack. He hitched up his pants and took a deep breath, "Maybe we need to replace the advisor."

"Do whatever you think is necessary." Sloan got up and started for the door.

"Ian." Chest deflated, pants drooping, jacket askew, face a multi car wreck. "Look...I didn't mean to be so abrupt...I...of course I wouldn't try to censor the *Roar*. It's just...there's so much going on now with Open House coming up. I really want everything to go off well, we all do…we don't need…do you think you could speak to her? Maybe, I don't know, tone it down a little?" Sloan wanted to tell him what a poor, pathetic bastard he was. Pathetic people everywhere he turned, including himself.

"I'll talk to her."

# NINETEEN

The street was full so he had to drive around to the parking lot in the rear. He expected a parade of wrecks, unkempt vehicles reflecting unkempt lives, but several were new, or near new, certainly newer than his. How could they afford them? Living in a dump like this? Of course, that explained it. Live like a peasant, drive like a king.

A black metal staircase, the steps ridged for better traction when it rained, led up to the back entrance. The appendage seemed more formidable than the building itself, a two-story block of sandy brick, which a strong quake would reduce to a dusty pile, leaving behind the dark ascent to nowhere.

On the landing a man in his fifties, leather vest on bare chest and a Raiders cap, stood smoking a pipe, one arm resting on the railing, eyes focused on an unremarkable sunset, a milky vista not yet allowing for stars. The watcher ignored Sloan until he got to the top of the stairs and without looking at him said, "Can't park there overnight without you got a sticker." His gaze remained fixed on the horizon. A tattoo on the upper arm, a clipper ship under full sail with lettering below, the word lost in the weathered skin. He had spoken with managerial authority, but the old man said the manager was a woman. The Pollack? Possibly. He looked the type who'd have a gun in his room. A shotgun.

Two barrels. Under the bed. A surly manic depressive who one night would, for whatever reason, dissatisfaction with a sunset or a football result, go berserk and create several vacancies.

"I'll only be a few minutes."

The sentinel drew long on the pipe stem. "Don't matter to me."

The pungent scent of curry filled the hallway. Two children playing with a race car on the dirty carpet before an open door looked up startled. Eyes luminous in thin, dark faces, hair glossy and thick and black, black as the staircase. The eyes grew larger as he approached. The roar of the engine ceased as he came near. The boy snatched the car and disappeared into the room, but the girl remained seated, cross-legged on the filthy carpet, expressionless as he passed.

He was uneasy inserting the key, felt guilty, as if he were violating something or someone. When it didn't immediately catch, he experienced a real unease. No one knew who he was. What if the Pollack came along with his gun...a stranger fumbling with the old man's door...no, someone would recognize him, would have seen him with his father... but what if...the bolt clicked loose and he stepped quickly across the threshold, closed the door, and paused to survey the room before fastening the chain.

The bed in its usual state of confusion, a pair of pants draped over the armchair. An open can of condensed milk left on the drain board, probably the same one from his last visit. He emptied the contents and ran water over the white ooze. A jar of instant coffee and a half loaf of bread stood near the hotplate. Meager provisions. Reminded again the significance of a meal at Everett's, he regretted not having taken him more often.

Four corner screws and a larger one in the center. He had the knife in hand when he remembered the old man's admonition and followed the cord to the outlet behind the headboard. He had to get down on his hands and knees and stretch his arm at an awkward angle to reach the plug.

"Jesus!"The plug did not release. He pulled harder and felt a twinge in his shoulder. He wiggled it back and forth until it pulled loose, his hand snapping back against the headboard. "Shit!"

He arose stiffly, a catch in his chest, and sat for a moment on the edge of the mattress. The fact was he too was getting older. He resolved to get some exercise.

The blanket had been pulled back exposing the wrinkled sheets and he thought of the many hours the old man had spent in slumber while the world outside below his window went on without him. And in an instant he understood, felt the pull of the bed, the desire to burrow down under the blanket, to bury his consciousness among the pillows. The primal urge for the fetal position. The homeless heeded the call on benches, in doorways. The lure of oblivion.

Both knives were dirty. He ran water over the one with the butter stain and dried it on the soiled dishtowel. The first screw popped free and a cockroach scurried out from the shadows. He could feel the roll but his fingers, large and stiff, inconsequential in the narrow space, could not quite grasp it. He removed another screw and lifted the bottom of the plate and drew the bills forward with his index finger. Mostly hundreds and fifties, tightly wound. The smooth, clean texture and official scent of newly minted currency. Almost thirteen hundred.

He was counting out the rent when he sensed someone in the hall right outside the door. Holding his breath, he tiptoed to the entrance and listened to the receding steps slow and measured. He eased the door ajar, one hand on the chain so it would not rattle.

An elderly woman gripping an aluminum walker turned ever so slowly and caressed the back of an elaborate blond wig. A scarlet smudge arched up to generous mascara, a painted calamity, and whispered a throaty, "Good evening, Mr. Sloan."

He set aside the rent, plus fifty for Pepe and slipped the roll back behind the cover. The second screw refused to take hold, twice dropping from the tip of the knife. Still he persisted, patient, concentrated, his reasoned, mature self telling him he was ridiculous. One screw, ten screws, what did it matter? Who would think to look in the back of a radio, especially in place like this? Yet the little boy, long schooled to obey, to do what he was told, to please, soldiered on until finally the screw fell to the floor and Ian Sloan, mature, independent thinker, kicked it into the corner. "The hell with it."

He struggled with the suitcase, a large, awkward container, stuffed under the bed and, catching it on the bedpost, was once again on his hands and knees to pry it loose. Inside an old shirt and three unmatched socks. Under the shirt an envelope, and scribbled in pencil on the back: "I know I hurt you little girl. But I'm finished with the drink." No name. No address. No date. Had he intended to mail it? An envelope within an envelope. Or simply an unburdening, a contrition not dispatched.

The closet held a sparse wardrobe. On the floor in the back, his dress shoes, his one great extravagance covered in dust. "*Fine shoes are like good manners, Lad. They show the quality of the man.*"From the ground up, the little things, the details, that marked a true gentleman. That was his father: considerate, gracious, well-mannered with all…but his own.

He remembered the day they purchased them. The shoe department, designated "Shoe Salon" in gold lettering above the entrance, pleased the old man. They sat on cushioned chairs while a neatly attired young clerk attended to his father, who clearly savored every moment. No slouching, dignified, he had worn a necktie and jacket for the trip. And when Ian brought additional styles from the displays for consideration, his father rejected them out of hand, not wishing to be seen as demanding, fussy, lording it over the clerk. A true gentleman knew instinctively how to conduct himself in any circumstance and, above all, was never condescending.

Yes, this was the life he was meant for: exclusive stores, quality footwear, fine clothes. He held the package discreetly as they strode from the salon and lectured Ian once again on the importance of good manners, of keeping your shoes shined and bemoaned an unjust fate that granted the unsophisticated, the uncouth, lesser mortals such indulgence, such luxury stolen from more deserving ones such as he.

*"Always the way, Son. Bloody guttersnipes, crooked bastards. They get it all. The honest, hard working man gets nothing...goddamn Jews."*

An old refrain, the spewed bitterness that accompanied them home and he remembered wanting to ask his father did he think you just parachuted into a life of ease and comfort. If wanting were enough, the entire world would be comfortable. And knowing how to use a knife and fork, knot a tie, fill out a suit, did not alone grant entry. Yes a boor in splendid dress was still a boor, but at least he had earned his drapery.

He had wanted to tell him that real gentlemen dragged themselves from bed in the morning and stayed home Saturday nights with their families, with the one woman. *"Your father has his faults, Ian, but one thing you can be sure of — he's a man of morals,"* his mother's oft repeated mantra which as Ian matured began to ring hollow. And real gentlemen did not drink away their wages, never raised their hand to their children.

The cardigan they had given him on Father's Day many years ago. Kelly green; he seldom wore it. The shade too conspicuous, too showy. He preferred gray or navy. Two shirts, their collars frayed, and a jacket. A half dozen ties strung from a coat hanger, one he recognized as a gift from Teddy. A rust color the old man insisted was orange, "bloody Orangeman's tie." He never wore it. From the doorknob hung a full laundry bag.

On the closet shelf an old Racing Form, opened to the fifth race at Hollywood. Selections marked with notations Ian interpreted as later odds and projected orders of finish. Same for the others, though nothing at all marked for the third, seventh, or eighth. The old man never played every race, concentrating only on those that offered the best odds and the highest probability. Anyone could play heavy favorites.

Once he had taken the train to Del Mar and placed only three wagers." *Never bet for the sake of betting."*

And always reserved seating. A better class of people he insisted. He felt more at home among his kind. He disdained the yelling of the railbirds, all that screaming down the stretch. With him you never knew the result: first, last, photo finish, long odds in – the expression remained fixed, placid throughout, an Island of equanimity. "The Sport of Kings." He belonged. The others, the General Admission crowd, interlopers, riff raff. *"Bloody low class. Guttersnipes."*

Often, he would delay the cashing of a ticket to a later date if the track was especially crowded so as to avoid the jostle of the mob. He did not wish to mingle, yet politically his sentiments had always been with the common man. Roosevelt the finest president. A devoted Democrat from the time he set foot in the States, though he had never bothered to become citizen, had never cast a ballot.

The wool cap he wore even in summer, on a hook inside the door. A checked pattern of gray and blue and tucked inside the rim a holy card. Saint Christopher on one side, "The Wanderer's Prayer" in elegant script on the other: "Dear God the Father Almighty, Guide my steps and light my way so that I might never…" Ian stared at the card. A revelation. Like living one's life behind a high wall and then on a whim one morning climbing a tree and viewing for the first time a vast panorama of fields and hills and river – always there, but never seen.

He replaced the card inside the band and returned the cap to the hook. Eleven years in the same room. A wanderer in place.

His hand on the doorknob, he took one last look around and the truth came to him, had been with him the moment he stepped into the room: neither he nor his father would ever return to this place.

He retrieved the money from the radio and did not bother to lock the door behind him.

He was built like a football player or one of those Eastern European weightlifters, expressionless grunters, who performed their feats and promptly departed. But the eyes were uneasy, cautious.

"Pepe?"

The young man hesitated before uttering a barely audible, "Yes," looking beyond Ian as if there might be another in the dimly lit hallway,

"Mr. Sloan, in the next room? He's my father." Pepe's face brightened, the thin mustache stretching, a pencil line, above his smile. A tiny earring caught the glint from the bulb in the ceiling above the door.

"Yes, yes…Mr. Sloan…such a good man. How is he?"

"Not too well, I'm afraid. He's very sick."

"Oh…that's sad, so sad." Pepe frowned but was more at ease. "Come in, please." He stepped backward with a lightness and grace that belied his bulk and nodded at a youth in floral underwear stretched out on the double bed. "That's Raoul." Raoul was fair skinned, clean shaven, and noticeably thinner than his roommate. He raised his head lazily from a comic book to acknowledge Ian. Next to the bed was a canvas beach chair and card table upon which were textbooks, paper and pens. "Everybody miss your father. 'Doctor Sloan' we call him. A very much gentleman."

"I just wanted to thank you for helping him. He told me you drove him to the hospital."

"S'no problem."

"He wanted me to give you something…to show his gratitude for all you've done."

"No. No. S'not necessary," said Pepe, his eyes fixed on the bill, uncertain of the denomination.

"He insists…You're a student?"

"Yes." Pepe glanced over at his makeshift desk, but was drawn back to the money. "I study civil engineering." Ian offered the $100.

"Too much! Too much!" cried Pepe, but he held fast. Raoul, having put aside the comic book, looked on with interest.

"He wanted you to have it."

"Your father is such a good man."

"Well…I have to go. I didn't mean to interrupt your work."

"S'no problem. Please tell your father 'thank you' and we want him to get better fast. Raoul and me we miss him." Raoul nodded again. "Everybody miss him."

The night gave up the strip of pavement to lamps that beckoned as Ian wove his way across the bridge.

Everything ended. All was fleeting. Jobs. Marriages. Lives. His father's soon. Sometimes he wished he too could end it. Not life necessarily, though at present he felt no great attachment, but his way of life. He was tired of teaching. He wanted to flee, but to where? A dreamscape of purpose and purity, a rejuvenation of the spirit, a reinvigoration? Not to be. No Shangri Las, only in the movies.

Unlike many, he had simply drifted into the profession. He was not out to save the world. The pay was not great, but at a certain point you could not easily leave it and find something comparable. Sure, there were intangibles. He was a good lecturer, some might even say inspiring, and in those first years he was genuinely touched when he knew he had affected them. And even now, he had his moments. But the lecture approach was coming under increasing fire. Uniformity was winning the day, teaching by the numbers. And given the broader context – the politics, the administrative self interest, the low expectations, the rationalization of laziness and irresponsibility, and, of course, meddling parents – not surprising more and more veterans, those once so nobly called, now sought only the Promised Land: the magic 63. Full benefits. Workshop in the garage, gardening, a little travel, and pray no illnesses. Then the vast imponderable.

In the rear view mirror the lamps shrunk, their glow receding as the bridge slipped away. The end. In education they called it "closure," the completion of a lesson, as did victims' families at state executions.

# TWENTY

"Listen up, people. Layouts are due at the end of the period. If you're not done, back after school until you finish. Remember, we come out Friday." Sloan returned to his desk and awaited the crises. Archie's was first.

"Mr. Sloan, Alice wants to pull one of my ads. She says she needs more space, but she can't do that. I have to run that ad." Archie began rubbing his teeth – the uppers only. An annoying habit that seized him whenever he was under pressure, and with Alice Trimble, Sports Editor, staring at him, his finger was getting a workout.

Alice came lumbering over, a big girl in peasant blouse, jeans and boots. She wore hoop earrings and several bracelets on each thick wrist. Sloan had met the mother a Back-to-School Night, an attractive woman around his age, a product of Sixties Berkeley who had retained the aura of social indignation. Bright, articulate, she had wanted to know to what degree he would be incorporating cultural diversity into his lessons. What minority writers would they be reading? And what of women writers? There were several she could suggest.

She had him, of course. What could he say? "Not interested, thank you." He had met variations of Mrs. Trimble before, but she seemed the very prototype of the high end Anesthesia parent:

educated, professional, complacent, the world a better place for her presence, and a desire to be heard. And Back-to-School Night and Open House, among others, provided the idea opportunity. Convenient arrangements under the guise of parent involvement. What better forum for the deeply dissatisfied, the impotent task-masters, the wreckers of their own lives. Administrators, teachers, all compelled to listen. From his experience, the more vocal the parent, the more dysfunctional the family. But they had their whipping boy – public education.

Alice was her mother's foil. A plain, unattractive girl, reticent, prone to surliness, and of only average ability. A shot-putter on the track team, she lived for sports and absolutely no interest in social issues.

"Alice, why do you need more space?" She glared at Archie as if she might heave him across the room, a record toss. The ad manager was rubbing vigorously.

"Athlete of the Month," she said, looking daggers at the ad manager. "I need two more inches. Julie said it's okay."

"Mr. Sloan, it's a new ad. I have to run it. They already paid. Incense Are Us, the New Age bookstore on Fairmont. It's a good account, Mr. Sloan. They'll buy space in every issue next year. I know they will. The owner graduated from Anesthesia."

"Alice?"

"I don't know anything about that. I need the space for my story," she said with the steely determination of a shot-putter calculating distance.

"And Archie's obligated to run his ad." Archie closed his mouth and put his hands in his pockets. "Can you cut your story a little?" Affronted, head high, an imperious Alice gazed at the relaxed, newly confident adversary. A little too confident, thought Ian. Might she be sizing him up, deciding which wall to bounce him off. There was no surrender in Alice. Compromise, possibly, but no surrender. Archie hadn't a clue.

"I cut almost a hundred words already. It's a lot shorter than our usual tribute."

"Archie, can you move the ad to another page, dump something else?"

"I…guess I could move it to Features. Drop Walker's Video, maybe. They're about the same size. He's a dork…never pays on time."

"Good. That's what we'll do then. Tell Julie and tell her I want to see her."

"Well, Alice, you're all set now." The Sports Editor had prevailed, but nothing in her suggested triumph as she trudged away without a word.


"Mr. Sloan, Archie said you wanted to talk to me." She held a legal pad in one hand, a pen in the other.

"You look like you're ready to take dictation." She offered a weak smile. No one dictated to Julie Fanning.

"How's everything look?"

"We'll make it. Eugene's having trouble with a headline for the PTA story and Melissa can't find a candidate profile but she's sure it's at home. She's going home at lunch to check."

"And if she doesn't?"

"I've already sent a call slip for him to come here at lunch. Melissa can interview him and write it up in study hall. She has his picture. I'll start the interview and she can take over when she gets back."

"Did Archie tell you about the ad change?"

"Yes, that will work."

"What's the latest on the pool?"

"He wasn't very cooperative, Mr. Sloan." A flutter, the indigo stream was rising. "He kept me waiting for about twenty minutes. His door was open and I could see there wasn't anyone there and he wasn't on the phone…he was hoping I would leave. I know."

"What did he have to say?"

"Not much but he admitted there was no bidding on the contract. First, I started by asking about the service, you know, what the pool people did. How often they came. He was happy to answer those questions, but he wasn't very clear about what they actually did. He just kept saying how the district was really satisfied with the quality of the work. But when I asked him how much it cost, he said he couldn't remember off hand. He said he'd look it up and let me know." She flipped back two pages. "I took a recorder too. I wanted to make sure I got everything down just the way he said it. I wrote a few impressions while he was talking." She had read somewhere that traditional journalists, the real pros, scorned recorders, so she rarely used one. "I told him I could wait while he looked up the information. He got a little mad, I could tell." Slimy though Vincent was, Sloan felt sympathetic. She was a shark. "He said it was impossible to check at the moment."

"You're tough."

"Mr. Sloan, you should have seen him. As soon as I turned on the recorder, he started getting…I don't know…nervous, kind of touchy. Then later he tried to change the subject. Acting all friendly and everything. Asking about my college plans, what I wanted to do, all that stuff."

"Maybe he was genuinely interested."

"He just wanted to get rid of me."

"He doesn't know Julie Fanning." She ignored the comment.

"I asked him if the District got quotes from other pool services and he said it wasn't necessary. They got a very good deal, better than other schools. Then I asked him how he knew that if they didn't get bids from any other company." She stopped to look at her notes. "When I asked him if his nephew owned the company, he got really upset. No more Mr. Nice Guy. He said that had nothing to do with anything and got up and said he had another appointment and couldn't give me any more time."

"Now what?"

"I left room for about 350 words. I've cut, but I'm still a little over. Do you want to see what I've written?"

He read slowly, but nothing registered. He was thinking how he would tell her. Ultimately, with Julie the best route was the direct one.

"Julie, I want you to hold off on this for the time being."

"Why? What's wrong?" She was stunned, the distress in her voice evident. "Don't you like it?"

"No. No…Yes, I like it, what you have is fine. But if you wait it will give you time to …sort of digest everything. And Vincent will probably get back to you on the cost."

"I can just go ahead with what I've got. He won't give me any information, I know he won't…probably won't even see me again." The strip below the eye quivered. She lowered her head and began flipping the note pages back and forth. He hoped she would not cry, not her. She looked up at him, eyes full. "The next issue is the last. I won't be around to follow up." She turned her back on him.

"Julie."

She spun around, clutching the pad to her chest. The dike had held. "Did anyone from the District call you?"

"No, of course not. Don't be silly." She scrutinized his face and suddenly he felt a brother to the Assistant Superintendent. "Have you ever considered police work?" She was not amused.

"Are they putting pressure on you?"

"For God's sake, this isn't exactly Watergate." The regret was immediate. Hit a kid and he'll heal. But words…You could undo, redo, correct, compensate, but you could not unsay. To belittle her passion was unforgiveable. "Julie, sometimes, for various reasons, it's what you don't write, what you don't do, that's significant." Christ! Did he just say that? Dialogue from a bad movie. A second rate Mr. Chips. He could easily imagine a student explaining a missed essay with the same line.

"We won't drop it. Trust me." She was still skeptical but the eyes had drained. "I'll tell you what. Call some other schools in the meantime. See if you can find out what they pay. Tell them who you are but try not to say anything about what you're writing. Be vague. If you can get some numbers, that will give you an idea of the going rate, then you'll have something to compare if Vincent gets back to you. You'll have more ammunition. The story will be stronger."

"But it will be the last issue." He knew he had her. She would never give less than her best.

"But this will be your best editorial. You'll go out with a bang."

"If you say so."

# TWENTY ONE

May. A woman's name. A waitress. A chain smoker. A drinker. May Day. Tanks on parade. Kremlin dignitaries, creviced faces in strained smiles from Red Square balconies.

Pinatas, mariachi bands, olive-skinned girls in flowing skirts and round-necked, cotton blouses. May was also spring. Flowers. Bouquets. In his youth the scent of lilacs. An intimate, sensual fragrance. Lilacs persuaded romance, but a short lived bloom.

Less than six weeks, not counting finals. A winding down. Seniors a study unto themselves. Paths had been determined; the remaining days, life in abeyance, on some high plain waiting. Nothing more to be done but savor accomplishment or lament failure. The former, the especially energetic, disciplined, resolute ones, bulging acceptance letters from their first-choice universities, others a scattering of rejections, but ultimately a school for each.

For the latter, the unaspiring, the jokesters, the confused, the realization, though unspoken, that clothes and cliques and parties were now meaningless. Lost opportunity. The enduring fork in the road, each set aware of the divide but neither acknowledging it. An unsettling truth never addressed. For the one a bright vista of accomplishment, security, comfort, possibly wealth, for the other a rutted track of mediocrity, limitation, poverty even. The illusion of equality in those sunshine early years, gone. From now on, only winners and losers.

He sighed as he pulled into the parking space. Commencement would close out another year, but graduations had become more and more dispiriting to Sloan, increasingly false ceremonies: honors cajoled, feted altruism born only of the college application process, diplomas awarded but many not really earned. Duplicity, connivance, a fabric woven without shame. A preview of what was to come? Yet there were the Julies – successes untarnished, achievement earned, grounded in character, offering hope for the future. But they had become so few, so very few.

Last Saturday he had shopped elsewhere, but he could not avoid her indefinitely he told himself as he grabbed a cart and headed for the produce section, making a point of not even glancing toward the checkout stands.

He was placing apples into a plastic bag when his heart began to flutter, then race. He tried to ignore it. A skipped beat, then another. He stopped and gripping the cart handle with one hand, apple in the other, he waited until it resumed its usual booted pattern. He had experienced rapid heartbeat before, but the skipping, the irregularity, were recent developments. Were they a signal, a warningl? He reviewed the symptoms: Pain or tingling in the arm? No. Shortness of breath? Not really. He was breathing hard whenever he got to the top of the stairs in his building, but that had always been the case and he had managed the trek to the bridge. Exhausted, sure, but no harm done. After all, he was middle age. Yet that catch in his chest when he stretched to unplug the old man's radio. And last year, just before Christmas, alone in his room at the end of the day. It came on him without warning, a nauseousness and his mouth filled with saliva, like a faucet turned on. Too much for his handkerchief. And Vivian Shelby, who in the spirit of the season was about to wish him good cheer when she saw him spit into the shrubbery outside his door, recoiled in disgust, though not in the least surprised.

But what if it was the real deal? He imagined himself prone at the base of the Washington delicious bin and the last thing, the last image of this time on earth would be a tearful Grace, bending over him in her uniform, her name tag and badges and pins and great breasts pressing down on him, her mouth searching for his.

He hurried from the produce section. In dairy he picked up a quart of low fat and passed on the extra sharp cheddar. He dallied in the farthest reaches, delaying the inevitable. He was being ridiculous he told himself. What could she possibly do? She might be angry him, but she wouldn't make a scene. She wasn't the irrational type, or was she? He barely knew her. Finally, he braced himself and turned down the coffee/tea aisle. As good as any. They all emptied out to the checkout stands.

She was the express checker and saw him as soon as he emerged. She gave a wide, arcing wave and grinned, as though she were marooned and he a passing vessel. A good sign. From the beginning he had pegged her as good-natured and forgiving. The three customers in line turned to toward him and seemed on the point of waving too. He smiled and hung a left into canned goods.

Diced tomatoes, sweet corn, peas, beets, anything. He kept dumping into the cart. By the end of the aisle, he had more than doubled the "ten items of less." On to the magazine rack to compose himself.

*Time, Sports Illustrated, House Beautiful, Guns and Ammo, . . . Morticians Monthly* if need be. Anything to delay his fate. He soon wearied of sharing space with three kids and a skateboard flipping through Rock magazines with attendant sound effects. One with a stunted ponytail played spasmodic phantom guitar to the delight of his companions.

Whatever happened to the days when kids pored over sports magazines? Already a month into baseball season. They should be checking stats. When he was a kid Opening Day was an event and summers meant baseball: playing it, watching it, listening to it, reading about it. The numbers of summer – the box scores. They knew the leaders in each category: home runs, batting average, rbi's, era's. Always a ballgame. You couldn't walk down a street without hearing the play-by-play from someone's garage or front porch or open car window. Batter vs pitcher, mind and body, that coordinated struggle in which each contestant sought to define the other, as well as himself, in those few seconds of intense concentration that excluded all but one another – the private contest in public. Strikeout! Those mighty swings at nothing, leaving behind a string of "if onlys" to grip the imagination. The groundouts, the flyouts, the supporting cast. Then the moment, the ultimate high drama when the white sphere shot off the bat, the crackling reverberation of ball on wood, no pinging echoes then, a rocket ascent into azure space, the announcer's voice, "Going, going" tracing its projection to that exhilarating moment, that grand denouement – "Gone!"

Upper deck. Mick, the Bronx Bombers. Across the summer ball fields of his youth they dug in at the plate and cocked the bat just like Mickey, faded back on long flies and risked embarrassment attempting Willie's basket catch, stood the mound with Spahn's aloofness, knelt on deck like the regal Williams. The game, the royalty: the ungainly Yogi, Hammerin' Hank, Stan the Man, so many. Each with an identity. They were of a different realm, yet you felt connected, felt you knew them.

Nobody wanted to be a rock star then.

An older man, in suspenders and a cut off t-shirt engrossed in a muscle magazine, flipped pages as if searching for someone. No hesitation. He knew what he was looking for and so did Sloan: the female bodybuilders. Clearly an aficionado. Muscle and sex. He lingered over a bevy of firm breasted, tight bunned, thick thighed wonders.

"These are some babes, huh?" He held up the magazine to share his find.

"Yeah, they sure are."

"Yep, these are babes. They can pin me anytime. I wouldn't mind. No, siree." He snapped a suspender. "Do any lifting yourself?"

They were both absorbed in discussion, the other checker, younger, thinner, in green-framed eyeglasses. When she saw him, Grace covered her face with a TV Guide; her associate staring at him and laughing. He assumed he of the limp dick was the topic.

The same at school, the casual talk of sex, as though it were a game, a diversion like any other. So pervasive, so nonchalant. Just last week at lunch he passed a group sitting in front of the auditorium, a squeaky voice narrating something about a hot bath afterwards. Ninth graders, not long removed from Barbie, recounting the intimacies of weekend encounters. Adulterated adolescence.

And the older girls who congregated at the tables outside the cafeteria in their excessive makeup, their mature hips and breasts carrying the weight of experience. The suppleness of youth having already faded, what remained? By twenty-five, thirty, untimely slipping into middle age with nothing to look forward to but food and television. He felt a twinge of sadness whenever he passed them on campus In his time all were virgins though pretending otherwise. Parroting one another's fabrications, they were, in fact, fortunate to get a feel, a little skin. One kid, Victor Schultz, with bad posture and no neck, kept a condom in his wallet which he flashed in study hall. The same one he carried all year, but the younger boys listened, impressed when Victor advised them to be ready when opportunity came knocking. But despite his preparedness, Sloan knew Victor's opportunities were slim and none. He was probably still carrying the rubber.

"Ian." Her line was empty and she was beckoning him over. He adopted a resigned air and pointed to the express sign above her register. "Ian" she repeated, a mating cry from across the check stands. He shrugged and indicated his basket, but the scent would not be denied. Out from behind the counter she charged like a rutted moose and straight for him.

"It's okay. I don't have no customers." She grabbed the front of his cart and dragged it with him in tow. They arrived simultaneously with a burly fellow who could have stepped right out of one of the muscle magazines, bulging biceps, a babe on each shoulder. A man Old Suspenders could appreciate. Sloan motioned for him to move ahead. He stared at Ian and then the cart before putting down his yogurt and mineral water.

A few items, that's all he had wanted, a simple, quick transaction, yet here he was, the object of scorn from someone who resembled a concrete barrier, the kind erected on the sidewalk before government buildings.

He watched for her reaction to the Rambo impersonator. There was none. She promptly gave the man his change, bagged the water and yogurt without so much as a "paper or plastic?" option. Grace could be decisive, She knew what she wanted. Much to his surprise, he felt vaguely pleased.

"Hi, stranger!"

"Hi."

"Haven't seen you in awhile. Where you been hiding?"

"Oh,…you know, busy." He kept his head down engrossed in removing the items from his cart, stacking them neatly by food group, while Green Frames at the next check stand strained to catch the exchange.

"I was thinking, 'How come he hasn't called?' Course, I'm so dumb. I forgot, I didn't give you my number. Here, before I forget." She tore a piece of discarded register tape and scribbled the digits. "You could have just dropped by." She feigned rebuke with a familiarity that depressed him. "Now there won't be no excuses." She tore off another piece. "What's yours?"

"I…I don't have one."

"You don't have a phone?…Why not?"

"Well, I do…but it's disconnected."

"Tell me about it…miss a payment or two, and bam! You pick up the phone one day and nothing. And it costs so much to get reconnected. They really stick it to you."

"No…I had it disconnected." A can of stewed tomatoes remained suspended above the scanner.

"Why?"

"I…I was getting crank calls."

"What kind of calls?" The stewed tomatoes remained aloft.

"Obscene calls," he said quietly. Jesus! What was he doing? Why didn't just tell her the truth, tell her he wasn't interested.

"Really?" She set down the can and leaned close to him "A woman?" she asked in a husky voice.

"Uh,…no. A man."

"A man!" She emitted a laugh/belch. "Scuse me…Wow!" Green Frames scanned a bag of salted mixed nuts twice. "Any idea who it is?"

"None at all." His mother was right. She always told Pety and him not to lie. Not only was it wrong, but once you did, there was no turning back, one built upon another until it all came crashing down.

"So it could be someone who knows you or a complete stranger."

"I have no idea."

"Maybe one of those Hollywood boys saw your cute little toosh and fell in love." She was clearly enjoying herself.

"Maybe."

"Well, don't worry, I'm not the jealous type. Let me know when you get it connected again." She drew nearer again. "I had a good time."

"Yes…I did too." He fumbled for his wallet. "How much?" She had not hit the total key. Where was everybody? The other registers had lines, why not hers?

"$21.15…Why did you leave so early? I wanted to make you breakfast."

With the passing days he had eventually arrived at the point where, though unable to completely forget, he could at least banish the entire episode to some dark corner of his consciousness, like the grotesque painting or knick knack acquired in a lapse of judgment and hidden away, too embarrassing for the trash bin even.

The immutable fact remained, though. Beneath the decorous uniform, striped and buttoned to the throat, the great tits accused. Though proper now, he had know them unbound, as he had that mountainous, white ass. They had shared a bed, naked, skin on skin, yet how did it come about? He still had trouble comprehending it. This creature with her gum and her service buttons. Had he some deep rooted psychological flaw only now surfacing? Anesthesia's own

Jekyll and Hyde. Dedicated educator by day, wanton fornicator by night, trolling supermarket aisles, haunting bridges in frenzied pursuit of the next sordid liaison. And he hadn't even had the satisfaction of a good fornication.

"Ben sure misses you."

"He's a terrific little guy. Say 'Hi' to him for me." He quickly pocketed the coins.

"Ian, would you do me a big favor?" He took a deep breath. What did "big" mean? So many people spoke in hyperbole, especially kids. They were like salesmen; you had to take what they said and divide by three. Then there were those rare pleas for which "big" did not nearly suffice; he feared this might be one.

"You remember Elway?" She gave him one bill.

"Ben's rabbit."

"Right." Another bill. Only two remained, half-way home. He could just grab them and run. "Elway's sick. He's been throwing up and crapping all over the place. Can't keep nothin' down. Just can't digest nothin'...know what I mean?"

"Yes,...I think so." Indeed he did. He wasn't feeling none too well himself.

"So I gotta take him to the vet. I'm gonna take a couple hours off Saturday morning...I got tons of sick time coming. Problem is Ben's so emotional about Elway. I can't take him with me. He'll get all upset and cry and my sitter can't make it 'til eleven so I don't know what... I was thinking...could you come by and take Ben out somewhere? The park...or the mall, or somewhere...just for a couple of hours, til I can get Elway to the vet and back without Ben knowing." She gave him the third bill but held fast to the last.

"I would but..."

"I know you probably like to sleep late on Saturdays and I'm sorry about that but...there's no one else I can ask." He could have pointed out to her that his being in the store was pure chance and... "Ben'd sure love to see you."

"What time?" She smiled broadly and released the last George. There it was then, a second career. No more teaching. Hostage negotiator par excellence. The key word was "negotiator"; he could free the hostage all right, but at what cost?

"You're a sweetheart...about 8:30. I'll tell Ben you're coming to take him out. He'll be so excited. Ben really likes you, Ian. And Ben don't just take to everybody. Ben's real particular.

# TWENTY TWO

The morning sunshine revealed exactly what he had expected. Night had masked the peeling paint, the dullness of beige and brown and the real dimensions, even smaller in their daylight clarity. No inviting glow from drawn windows, only blank frames caught in the morning glare. And the grassy rise more clearly dirt than grass. The 3 remained upended; the scooter, however, was neatly parked, perhaps in his honor.

Ben was ready in t-shirt, jeans, and sneakers.

"He's been standing at the door for the last half hour," said Grace, her lipstick tangerine, a direct repudiation of the pinkish shade she usually favored, the eyes highlighted, enlarged orbs that startled in their directness.

Ben took his leave of Helter and Skelter and Elway, but refused to nuzzle the rabbit. He held his nose and pointed at the afflicted. "Poo. Poo."

She slipped her arm through his and pressed close, glancing right and left at the passing doors, nodding acknowledgments as they made their way down the carpet between the velvet ropes, Cameras clicking. She loved her fans, so very grateful for their loyalty. Yes, she too thought it her best work in ages. No, they had only recently begun dating but both felt it was the real thing. True, she had always been fond of older men. The maturity. And they complemented one another so well: his intellect, her beauty.

"Morning, Helen. Morning, Alberta," she called to the two elderly women in white plastic chairs sunning themselves. "Everybody thinks they're lesys. They been here more than twenty years..." She returned their not-quite-adoring wave. "They probably are...there's only one bedroom...they're nice and...you know...to each his own, that's what I always say, but...I don't know, it's kind of yucky when you think about it...old ladies."

Curbside she picked Ben up and kissed him, then stepped toward Sloan. He turned to unlock the door. "What time should I bring him back?"

"About eleven." An energetic sendoff, the arms moving so vigorously one would have thought Ben and he were embarking on a Trans Atlantic crossing. All that was missing were the streamers. In the rear view mirror he watched her bulk, dock side, still wishing Godspeed as Ben and he turned the corner and set out to sea.

But where to go? What to do? He hated malls. Too early anyway, same with the movie theaters. That left only the park, but he didn't exactly relish the thought of an extended conversation with a two-and-a-half-year-old whose social experience was limited to two cats named after an infamous killer and a vomiting rabbit with the shits.

"Want to go to the park, Ben?"

"Park! Park!" He squirmed in his seatbelt.

Ben called to the docile ponies who waited patiently as the attendant prepared them for the day. A small group of families, mostly mothers, had already gathered at the ticket booth. Soon the animals would bear their writhing, screaming, crying loads with aplomb, resigned to the many treks around the ring. A reluctant, plodding walk, a canter at best. Ben would connect. Cats, rabbits, why not ponies? Ben was at one with his four-legged brethren, but Sloan dared not chance it.

184

If something happened to the boy…the prospect of a bereft Grace in black, her grip viselike; he could actually feel the pressure. He would owe and owe. The debt unpayable. He would never escape.

He hadn't been to Griffith Park in years. When Teddy was little, they took him at least once a week in summer. He would pad along among the horses and carriages searching for Pronto, the one with the chipped tail. He was fascinated by the exposed plaster. And afterwards they would sit on the grass under a tree eating hotdogs, Evelyn's slathered with mustard, relish, and onions…and never enough napkins.

He peered through the windshield searching for the merry-go-round sign. He saw it, just ahead, covered in graffitti.

At the conclusion of each ride, he gave the attendant another ticket, while Ben sat waiting, alternately pulling on the reins and hugging the neck. When they first got on, he sought out the chipped tail though after all this time it had probably been replaced. He seated Ben and strapped him securely, then lurched from pole to pole for one last look while the organ played "When I'm Sixty Four." Pronto too was gone.

The only other rider was a girl of uncertain age who sat in one of the three carriages with her grandfather. A bright blue ribbon bound her hair in a ponytail and she grinned blankly at the flitting images. Somewhere in that spinning world of colors and shapes was grandmother waving and crying "Marissa" with each revolution and only when the ride slowed and the carriage came around to his side, did Sloan understand the tilt of the head, the vacant eyes, the precarious steps, the easy joy.

Tall and dignified, with thick, gray hair and an air of contentment, her guardian took her hand, guiding her gently among the figures.

"Isn't it wonderful to be a grandfather?" said the man as he stepped down.

When they were walking to the car Ben, who had been toddling on ahead after a squirrel, returned to take his hand. The boy's touch

185

surprised him. He felt the pull of the little body and gazed down in wonder.

"Are you hungry? Want a hotdog?" He grinned and broke into a wobbly run singing, "Hotdog. Hotdog." Ben got right to the point. Like his mother, he knew what he wanted.

Ben wandered around the apartment, checking out the bathroom and bedroom, then returning to the living room where he crawled under the table and sat and farted while Sloan tucked his father's money into an envelope.

Grace was dressed for work and Elway was once again ensconced among his pellets. Ben went on breathlessly about the carousel and the ponies.

"I should take him there sometime. I never thought of it...I sure do appreciate it, Ian." She wrapped his name in new familiarity, a domestic intimacy.

"We had a good time. How's Elway?" At the sound of the name, Ben sped to the kitchen and out the back door.

"He'll be okay. Vet says it's some bacteria. I forget what it's called. I have to give him some medicine for a few days."

"I'm glad it's nothing serious."

"Naw, he'll be okay...and you know what?"

"What?"

"To show you how grateful I am, I'm going to cook you something really special." He started to protest. "Not Mexican. We're done with that...for now...I got lots of tasty recipes. You're looking at a chef, Mister, not just any old cook."

"Grace, I can't."

"Why not?" He heard the desperation; his heart fluttered and he felt short of breath. "Don't tell me you're married. Are you gay?

Naw,…not you." She chuckled, the laughter hollow." I know you're not married."

"No, it's just…It's just that I don't want…"

"I'm not trying to put any pressure on you or anything. I like everything the way it is with us…I know you…"

"No no. You don't understand…" He hated himself. Why had he… he understood too well her longing…the couples passing through her checkstand day after day in their selfish joy, their laughter, their embraces, their giving of themselves to a world of promise, women with children and men coming home while she joked and chatted and pretended a like future as she grew bigger and the walls more confining, until eventually a quarantine of hopelessness. He abhorred the unfairness, the inequality, and… himself for having become an accomplice to her cruel fate.

"Okay. I get it. Fine. No problem." She snatched her handbag from the couch. "Stupid me."

"Grace, I just don't want to get involved."

"Yeah, sure, no problem…Ben!"

"I wanted to give you this." He removed the envelope from his pocket. "I don't need it and…" She opened the flap and touched the bills.

"What's this for?"

"Just something…"

"What the fuck is this!" She shook the envelope at him. "You think I'm a fucking whore!" He cringed under the assault while Ben stood watching from the kitchen. "I mean I guess I should be flattered…I… especially since you couldn't even get it up." She threw the envelope across the room.

"It's for Ben." He started to gather the bills.

"Ben don't want your fucking money." She dashed into the kitchen where Ben, who had heard the commotion and come in from the rabbit cage, stood in the doorway, his lip trembling. She eased her way past him, as though on a tightrope, down the counter to the wall where she remained.

"...for his education...a savings account...if you can add a little each month, by the time he's eighteen..." He set the envelope on the arm of the couch and backed out the door.

# TWENTY THREE

"A Celebration of Uniqueness" the posters on campus proclaimed. The audience, a varied group, a few of whom refused to stand, pledged their allegiance, followed by a stout girl from choir who belted out an improvisational "Star Spangled Banner" that sounded more like stripped gears than a jazzy rendition.

Aztec dancers in dazzling costumes paraded across the stage in single file in an ancient tribute to the gods. Athletic boys, bare chests and legs beneath elaborate headdresses. Sloan recognized Carlos from his third period under the plumage. The first he had seen him all week. Punctual for Montezuma but a no-show for American Lit.

Next Korean dancers, all girls, gliding in bright, gauzy pant outfits and swirling, ankle length dresses. Many graceful runs, skips, and jumps to the eerie strains of a stringed instrument. Following them Edgar Fabrizzi, center on the football team, unshaven in tuxedo, burst into a selection from "The Barber of Seville." His Pavarotti imitation replete with handkerchief and much dabbing of the forehead.

The mood turned even more festive with the Celtic dancers, linking arms and kicking skyward, kilts swirling as they stepped nimbly. An elderly gentleman, someone's grandfather in the center front row, kept inching downward in his seat, tilting his head for a better view, assuming that in the darkened auditorium none would be the wiser. But a woman of equal years, no doubt another someone's grandmother, sitting directly behind, leaned forward and whispered into his ear, "You're D-I-S-G-U-S-T-I-N-G."

When he and Pety were little, they would cross a broom and a mop on the living room floor and render their version, skipping around and around, hands on hips and pester the old man was it true that Scotsmen wore nothing under their kilts, and he would tell them that yes it was so, explaining that in battle there was no time to stop and go to the bathroom and would give them a rare, strained smile, thin lips stretched above false teeth and strangely wonderful for its infrequency. But without the dentures and eyeglasses and disturbed from his Sunday nap the more familiar squinting, gap-mouthed monster up from the depths.

The doctors could not, or would not, predict how much time he had drifting in and out of consciousness, like a last guest reluctant to leave, though the cleanup had begun.

Awake, his father was alert, but speaking had become increasingly more difficult. Ian had called the local parish, Our Lady of Fatima, to make arrangements for last rites, a final confession, but was put on hold and told there was no one available. He would drop by the rectory tomorrow.

The old man was what the church politely termed a "lapsed Catholic," a non attendee, but Ian was certain, a break in practice only, not in faith. The number of his transgressions would prove daunting for any confessor. Still, his father stood firm on dogma. A last avowal, a devout act-of-contrition, and all would be forgiven, the prodigal returned from the very precipice of eternal damnation.

Along the east and west walls of the auditorium, members of the school's Christian Club had positioned themselves in silent protest, refusing to take seats. Each wore a black t-shirt embellished with a quote from Genesis in heraldic, white script and holding a placard that read "Jesus Is Our Savior."

They had petitioned Bengstrom to be a part of the evening's program, readings, hymns, and a dramatization, and though the principal was not personally opposed, he was advised there could be a backlash, legal action even. He denied their request in his most amicable fashion, even offering to pray with them at their next meeting, but they would not be assuaged and tabbed him. "Godless Bengstrom."

"The Great Dane" approached the dais.

"Here we go," said Roth, slouched in his seat. "Here come de schmaltz."

"Hang in there," said Sloan. "Remember, Open House means the end is near."

"Please, God, no props, no visual aids," said Roth. Last year the speech was "Roadblocks to Learning." Bengstrom had held up sticks of different lengths, the ends buried between his fingers but all the same height outside the hand that enclosed them to illustrate the unseen problems and anxieties of Anesthesia's young people. Hidden burdens, some heavier than others, but all deeply rooted obstacles to success. A kid in the back of the auditorium who had been expelled the week before and apparently deciding he had nothing more to lose, yelled, "Stick it in your ear!"

The evening's discourse, in keeping with the diversity theme, was entitled "The Family of Man." The principal descended from the stars to the planet, to the continent, to the country, to the region, to the state, to Anesthesia, to AHS. Early in his career he had taught "Our Town." But tonight he was in their town but lacking his usual bonhomie. He stood before them a pale and somber man of Scandinavian descent. His jacket was buttoned, but the desired formality was undercut by a binding sausage image whenever he gestured. When the perspective had reached the school, he paused, fumbling inside his jacket.

"Aw, shit," said Roth. "What'd I tell you. Watch this…great, a rope."

Bengstrom extended his arm to the audience, striking some in the Christian Club as a supplication, an offer of peace, but not Sloan. For him the droopiness of the dangling coil was simply an unpleasant reminder.

"A public hanging," said Ian. Louise Randall, a Bengstrom ally, cast a disapproving glance and whispered, "Sh."

"Like the strands of this rope," said the principal, "our students, faculty, and administration are bound together as one to achieve the same goal -…"

"Edible cafeteria food," said Roth.

"…the education and nurturing of Anesthesia's young people. And as with any family, there must be a strong leader, a strong father figure, unafraid to make difficult decisions and if you will…"

"A plea."

"You think he's out?"

"He's out," said Sloan. "They just haven't told him yet. He's history, sorry bastard."

"…and I have tried to provide that leadership and with your help will continue to do so as long as humanly possible."

Centered in the quad in long gowns and tuxedos, the choir, half of whom would be hard pressed to locate Scotland on a map, performed selections from "Brigadoon." A fairyland, a magical kingdom in the misty highlands. How Sloan wished he might fly there now instead of trekking to his classroom where a throng had already gathered at the door.

The citizens of Anesthesia knew their power on these occasions. This was their night, to roam the campus unfettered, acknowledged, catered to, the general obsequiousness of the staff reinforcing their sense of entitlement.

And all was for show: classrooms festooned with posters and graphs and banners, a variety of student work, but only the very best examples, and special lighting, gadgetry even. Please me, impress me, amuse me, the parents implied in their proprietary strolls, not unlike their offspring. He had once told Roth the district had it all wrong. Open House should mean the teachers get to go to the students' houses, see how the parents were holding up their end, check the kid's room, demand proof of study habits.

"Mr. Sloan?" A thickset man, early fifties, in an Italian sweater of fine, deep purple cashmere with discreet HW gold monogram offered his hand, "Harve Wexler." A businessman's grasp: firm, decisive, brief. "My wife Elizabeth." He nodded at the woman beside him. Sensuous lips granted a perfunctory smile. Cosmetically attractive, late thirties; certainly not the gaunt, frantic fiftyish woman who had introduced herself as Blaine's mother on Back-to-School Night in September.

"Hello, Blaine." The boy stood shoulder to shoulder with his father, a complacent grin, as if to say, "Now let's see you get on my case."

Sloan had noted in recent years that many of the students who were not doing well accompanied their parents to these functions. In an earlier time the marginal ones would never have dreamed of showing up. But fear, shame, were outmoded, disagreeable words that had long since succumbed to self esteem. A culture void of embarrassment. Increasingly, the kids ran the show and they knew it. Open House had evolved to entertainment, to payback, a chance to see a teacher cower.

"So how is Blaine doing?" An absurd question. All four knew how Blaine was doing. Report cards had gone out just two weeks prior, and Blaine's D- was as indelibly etched as, no doubt, were the other D's and F's he was getting.

"Not very well. Didn't you get his report card?"

"Yes, yes. Of course." He jerked his head back and stared at Sloan.

"Has he made any improvement?" said the new Mrs. Wexler, who had retrieved a pen and small pad from her handbag.

More arrivals milling around by the door, browsing at the texts and papers he had laid out on the table to keep them busy. Most knew each other and their kids. An opportunity to examine the competition, but casually, with an aplomb conveying that all was well in one's own backyard.

"Not much."

"Are your tests objective or essay?" Irrelevant. Blaine would fail each equally well he wanted to say, but he understood the dynamics. She uncovered the pen, a recording for posterity, a hint of legalese, intimidation, implied reprisal. And he should realize that she was not merely decorative. She was a good mother, responsible, concerned, albeit not a real one. Welcome to Fantasyland, to Brigadoon.

"Both. Each unit test has objective questions and an essay."

"Do you give homework every day?"

"Just about. But Blaine seldom does it, or does it half heartedly." Blaine's grin had evaporated. He was in unfamiliar territory.

"'Half heartedly.' What does that mean?" She was looking at him, not her hand, as she wrote. He should also recognize that she was bright, formidable, a woman to be reckoned with. What he did know was that whatever she was scribbling was illegible.

"Means with half-a-heart…little effort…shoddy work."

"Blaine, you said you were doing your homework." Mr. Wexler tried to reassert the executive persona.

"I do,…most of the time."

"Not yesterday," said Sloan. He was not in the mood for games.

"Blaine?"

"I started to, but I fell asleep. I was really tired."

"He has swimming practice every morning. Has to get up at five thirty," the father explained, as if the addendum settled the matter.

"Maybe he should give up swimming until his schoolwork improves." Dumbfounded, Blaine shook his head and exhaled in a torrent. Sloan wanted to smack him. That's all he really needed: a kick in the ass.

"Just a minute, young man. That is a distinct possibility." The boy was about to protest, but thought better of it. Neither the time, nor the place. Mrs. Wexler, interrogator poseur, had put away her tools. Sloan was beginning to enjoy himself but the crowd was getting restless.

"We can discuss this further if you'd like to set a date for a conference."

They affirmed they most certainly would. They would get back to him. Blaine slunk off. A temporary defeat only. At home, behind closed doors, he would rise from the ashes on the crest of the divorce guilt.

A slight Asian man strode purposefully toward him. Short, quick, steps, an unsmiling determined expression and for an instant an image from an old television clip came to mind. Japan? Korea? He couldn't quite remember. Many years ago. An assassination attempt caught on camera. Some event, a formal occasion of some sort. The assailant dashed across the stage toward the speaker and lunched with the dagger, a long blade that caught the man in the mid section. He could still see the victim, doubled over, clutching his abdomen. And now it was his turn, razor sharp, ripping through the shirt he had just bought and tearing into the chest, leaving him to bleed to death on his own classroom floor. His body in lieu of grade. All the Blaines would be avenged.

Without a word the face recast into a broad smile of gray/white teeth. Both hands grabbed one of Sloan's and pumped vigorously.

"Thank you, Mr. Sloan. Celia say you the best teacher. Thank you. Thank you very much. Thank you very, very much." He was captivated by the mole below the right ear and the three long black hairs that sprouted there, bobbing up and down, as though waving to him. Then, just as abruptly, the man released his grip and with a last "Thank you very much" hurried away, followed by Celia Tranh, one of his best students, a quiet Vietnamese girl new to the district.

The procession continued on through the evening. At one point he noted a rumpled Bengstrom loitering by the door. Stoop shouldered, jacket undone, pants slipping, disheveled almost. Sloan surmised the poor bastard had probably taken a beating all night. Yet he was still standing, making his case to a disinterested parent, while in the background the choir filled the night with "Old Man River."

# TWENTY FOUR

"Teddy's gone," she said with the finality of one for whom assertion is fact. "He's run away." She shuddered, sipped the diet soda, and with trembling hand replaced the tumbler on the glass top of the blue, metal table with matching chairs. The patio was used brick with a walkway that stretched down to the pool side, where four lounge chairs awaited. The palette purple of a jacaranda tree in full bloom lay scattered on the green turf below. These were the kind of places people ran to, he thought, not from." I haven't slept all night." Her pink eyelids bore witness. "And with Devon not home…it's been hard, Ian. Very hard." She compressed her napkin into a little ball and squeezed. "I know I look terrible, but I can't help it."

"You look fine. I think you're making too much of this. After all, he did call."

"He said he wasn't coming back."

"No, he said he wanted to stay away for awhile. All he said was he might not come back for a few days." She had played the message for him as soon as he arrived. "He'll be home soon."

"I tossed and turned all night. I couldn't eat. All I've had today is a soft-boiled egg. I keep imagining all kinds of terrible things. Teddy roaming around Hollywood, hungry, tired. And all those horrible, disgusting street people. Perverts and drug addicts…if anything happens to Teddy…"

"Evelyn, c'mon, be sensible. Why would he be roaming around Hollywood?" He wanted to laugh. "Anyway Teddy can take care of himself."

"He's just a child."

"He'll be seventeen next month."

"He's still a boy. He doesn't know…"

"Evelyn, these kids aren't like we were when we…when I was seventeen. They're more…worldly."

"Do you think I should call the police? I was going to and then I thought I better wait until I talked to you."

"He's not missing. I'm sure he's with friends. Anyway, I think you have to wait twenty four hours before you can report a missing person."

"I've called around but none of his friends say they've seen him. Maybe he's got new friends. Oh, Ian, I hope he isn't mixed up with a bad crowd."

"No. No. In fact, I don't think he's far away at all. Obviously he cares enough to call you and let you know he's all right. He doesn't want you to worry."

"Not worry! Of course I'm worried." She released the paper ball.

"Does he get along all right with Devon? Any problems, disagreements?"

"No. No. They hardly ever see each other…never any problem between them. That's why this came as such a shock. I can't understand it. I thought things were getting better. I don't know what you said to him but Teddy seemed to be a little easier…not as moody. I thought he was really coming around." She went silent for a moment, as though reconsidering a point or recalling a vital piece of information. "And we've planned a trip for summer…a train trip, first class…across Canada. Now, I don't know…we might have to cancel…When Devon gets back, we'll talk it all out… deposits and reservations and everything…I hope there aren't any problems…sometimes these things can get messy."

"Have you checked with his school?"

"I talked to his counselor this morning. He wasn't in any of his classes yesterday. Ian, I can't understand it. He has everything. I know we don't spend a lot of time, but like you said, he's almost seventeen. And he has his own friends. You know how kids are. And Devon…we're both so busy."

"He's probably just going through some kind of teen mid life crisis… questioning everything. That's normal. Healthy. Teddy's no fool." He thought he was at his reassuring best, sounded good to him, but she was gazing at her hands and did not respond. Slowly she turned one over and then the other. What more could he tell her? She was closer to the boy. She knew him better. Mothers enjoyed a special relationship that fathers could not enter. He had been excluded for a while now. "Teddy's not" he struggled, "self destructive in any way. I mean…" What the hell was he doing? She hadn't said anything about suicide. Oh, Christ! Please, no hysteria. He couldn't deal with that.

"I just don't seem to have any energy anymore. I have no interest in anything. I haven't been to the gym in two weeks."

"This business with Teddy has got you down," he said relieved.

"It's not just Teddy. I've been feeling like this for some time now." She retrieved the paper ball which had begun to unravel. "I feel like I'm slipping backward."

"Have you brought it up in therapy?"

"I'm not in group anymore," she said offhandedly, as one dismisses a dish not to his liking.

"What happened? I thought you were getting a lot out of it?"

"I was. But I've moved beyond the group. Group can take you only so far… Ian, how do you think I look?"

"Fine, why?"

"I mean for my age…Do you think I look good for my age?"

"Why are you asking me that?"

"Well, do you?"

"Yes…you do, sure you do."

"You're not just saying that?"

"No, honestly. You really do."

"Could I pass for late thirties?"

"Evelyn, what's this all about?" She touched the skin inside her upper arm, more delicate and lighter than the outer, and massaged gently.

"I think Devon's seeing someone…a younger woman." She continued to caress the arm with the palm of her hand, both seeking and providing reassurance.

"What makes you think so?"

"Just a feeling. Woman's intuition, a woman knows. He's away more and more. Working longer hours…men are always attracted to younger women. They're never satisfied. And Devon's still a pretty good looking man…I mean…for his age…many women would…"

"Evelyn, you're making yourself miserable."

"Look, I'm getting a double chin." She raised her head. "I'll end up just like my mother. A double chin, three chins,…"

"Evelyn, stop it. You look fine."

"No, I don't!"

The sun had set without preamble, an unremarkable descent. The jacaranda tree and the lounge chairs shadows of their former selves.

"I need a career," she pronounced calmly. "I'm not productive enough. I'm thinking about getting into real estate. I would only handle upscale homes, of course."

"Real estate's booming. Lots of money being made."

Both fell silent. Not the comfortable, familiar quiet when words are unnecessary, rather that awkward silence when they simply will not declare themselves and if they do, are of little value.

"Ian, would you say I have a good life?" She crossed her arms and held tightly, as if a part of her might escape.

"Yes, I'd say so. Beautiful house, nice car, clothes…and you have your health."

"But I'm not happy, Ian…I don't know why." As with his father, there was much he might have told her but it would serve no great purpose now. Besides, he did not want confidences. Revelation carried… obligation. The inner chamber opened, and one ceased to be a guest. Such familiarity belonged to the past. She waited, expectant.

"What do you want?"

"I don't know. It's crazy. Like you said, I should be happy. Other women in my position would be…I just don't know. What about you, Ian? Are you happy?"

"Happy as the next guy, I guess."

"What would make you happier?"

"What is this? Twenty questions?"

"No, really. Nothing seems to bother you. What do you want?"

"Not much I suppose…no complaints." He laughed and took her hand. "It's getting chilly. Let's go inside."

She insisted he stay for a light supper. A simple meal, pasta, salad, garlic bread, a little wine. She dug out an old photo album and they reminisced and laughed at themselves, he in hideous flared pants and she in a Mother Hubbard dress. A shot of Teddy sitting alone on the front lawn of the apartment building a few weeks before they moved into the two bedroom fixer upper. Teddy at four staring into the camera. Not amused, not surprised or frightened…alone, adrift in that space. The picture saddened him and when she went to kitchen for the coffee, he removed the snapshot from under the cellophane and tucked it inside his shirt.

He updated her on his father's condition, and she promised to try and get over to the hospital. He left reassuring her all would be fine and that he would call tomorrow.

He drove slowly down Foothill checking the mini malls on the off chance he might see Teddy. He slowed to study a group of boys at a gas station and rolled down the window. One of them saw him staring and said something to the others. In his rear view mirror he saw them dash into the street, laughing and gesturing, one boy grabbing his crotch and heard "old faggot" as he sped away.

# TWENTY FIVE

Midway he had already counted three rings, but his days of sprinting up stairs two at a time with an armload of books and a thermos had, like his hairline, gone south.

He had once read the results of a survey conducted in the days before answering machines which indicated that most callers gave up after the seventh ring having concluded their party was not home or was having sex. And he had so few calls anyway. Mostly his father, and he was an anomaly. He might wait, ten, twelve rings. The hike to the payphone at the end of the hall had grown increasingly more trying; sex or sex, the old man would not easily capitulate.

Answering machines made Sloan uncomfortable, and though he did not have one, everyone else did, especially concerned parents who were never home. And for him, leaving a message was an ordeal. When the beep sounded, he would hesitate, begin, pause, and start again, certain he sounded the fool. Then trying to salvage the disjointed communiqué' would conclude with an overly long response. Not exactly the best impression for one whose stock in trade was language: clarity, succinctness, coherence. On tape he was the palsied surgeon, unable to slice a pie even.

Dr. Tsai too was an aberration. Sloan picked up on the eighth ring; no trouble understanding this time. His father was fading fast; he would not last the night.

Peak visiting hours. A corridor of activity but no apprehension. Bright metallic balloons with happy faces. Baskets of cellophane-covered fruit and candy. Flowers. Cuddly bears and much optimism. In one room a solitary visitor sitting close, clasping a withered hand, listening. In another a family gathered in their good health, a collective effort, a rising current of life, laughter even. Grandma was doing better. From her pillows she held court. She was no slouch, giving them back their joy and then some. A Mardi Gras atmosphere. He half expected a string of gurneys, patients waving, tossing bedpans, untying gowns to moon the crowd. Not for them death's intrusion. In his father's wing all seemed to be recovering but him.

The television was on, the volume low. The old man was sleeping, his breathing uneven, a struggle in slumber.

"He was here earlier, but Mr. Sloan was sleeping. Father said he would come back later," a Filipino nurse in a gold necklace explained when he inquired about the priest. "I just got off my break. Let me ask…Lucia, did Father ever come back?" He recognized them as the weekend planners from his last visit.

"I don't think…I haven't seen him."

The priest he had met at the rectory was indifferent. Tall and thin, somewhat stooped, with a narrow, strained face, he had seemed annoyed by the request. Theology aside, Ian doubted such a presence would provide much solace anyway.

He made himself comfortable in the only chair on his father's side of the room. The other bed was still empty, tight, clean, awaiting the next occupant. Ian flipped the channels and settled on an old black and white movie, "The Informer," the Victor McLaglen film about the IRA.

A sweeping interior shot, chandeliers and stained glass, then to ground level. Slowly up the center aisle he staggered, sobbing, begging forgiveness, an overlay of violins. The statuary, the altar, and in the middle front pew a kneeling figure in black: kerchief, shawl, dress. Closeup: the covered head, the worn face, the appealing eyes. The typically long suffering Irish mother/wife, bony hands measuring the rosary, fingers working the beads, pale lips counting to heaven, mother of him whom Gyppo had betrayed, a preview for all the bright colleens then who might welcome a young man's blarney, wishing only to escape that island, that fate.

Cut to Jesus nailed on the cross.

Ian returned to the nurses' station and called Our Lady of Fatima rectory. A pleasant voice assured him he would be right over.

A doctor he did not recognize was listening at the old man's bare chest. His father was staring blankly ahead. Ian remained in the doorway, not wanting to interrupt.

"I'll be done in just a minute." He quickly buttoned the pajama top without looking at the old man and placed the stethoscope in the gown pocket.

"Are you a relative?" he asked when they had stepped into the hall.

"My father."

"You're Ian," he said, looking at his chart.

"Yes."

"Dr. Lasky." They shook hands. He was older, but not much, and radiated competence, intellect, and a burly health. A doctor who would inspire confidence.

A little cold, but competent, purposeful.

"I need to ask you," he said, looking at the chart again, "since your name is on record as the nearest relative…" The poise, the equanimity, wavered a little.

"Yes."

205

"Your father will probably slip into a coma soon and before long expire, unless he's put on life support…it is up to you…your decision whether to put him on life support." He spoke in the monotone of a mechanic giving an estimate, leaving the owner to decide whether the vehicle warranted the expense, and the garage was busy. When Ian did not immediately reply, Dr. Lasky began looking around. He nodded to passing staff and shifted the clipboard from one hand to the other.

"I…don't think so…if there isn't any hope…" Ian waited to be contradicted, to be offered a glimmer, but none was forthcoming. "No…he's too old."

"I had to ask. I'll check back later." He walked briskly down the hall, stopping to jot a note before entering another room. Would a similar offer be made there?

The old man was staring at the screen. How much longer before the eyes stopped seeing? The gravity of what he had decided suddenly struck Ian. These hours would be the last.

"Hi, Dad."

"Hello, Son," his father mouthed, unheard.

"'The Informer,'" said Ian, nodding at the television. "Victor McLaglen."

Simple-minded Gyppo was wandering through the damp, foggy Dublin night, shoulders hunched, hands plunged deep into pockets, clutching the Judas coins. Under a street lamp he stopped to squint at a trench-coated figure in the distance. He knew he was under surveillance. Defiant, he entered a pub and bought drinks for the house. They gathered at the bar and toasted Gyppo, a fine man indeed.

Ian turned to his father. "Good movie." The old man attempted a smile. McLaglen had been a fighter in his youth too, and according to the old man an able one. A heavyweight. He had the face and voice of an ex pug, lumpy and nasal. Gyppo stood another round and the crowd cheered. Was there ever a better man? If so, they'd like to meet him.

One night, late, Pety already fast asleep and the old man not yet returned, he kept vigil with his mother in the kitchen while she recounted a missed opportunity. The early thirties, the depths of the Depression, but his father was one of the lucky ones. He worked on the line at Ford, Joe Louis not fifty feet away. Who would have thought he'd be the heavyweight champion?

Ford sponsored a Saturday evening radio program, a variety show. His father represented the River Rouge plant, qualifying to compete against three other acts on the nation-wide hookup. All who heard him in those days agreed he had a grand voice, another John McCormick. He was to sing Irving Berlin's "Always," his mother's favorite.

He donned his blue suit, gray fedora, and new elevator shoes and boarded the bus for the studio downtown.

After the dishes, ten minutes to the hour, she sat down next to the radio, fiddled with the dials until satisfied with the reception, turned up the volume, and settled in with her tea. Anxious, filled with anticipation. He need not win. It was enough that he perform. He told her he would be singing just for her, for his darling Eileen. And she knew they would cherish the memory of that night forever, savoring it again and again as they grew old. So too would the boys, something to be proud of, to brag to friends as they grew up. And who knew what unforeseen good fortune might come as a result. One could always dream.

She suffered through the theme song and the opening ads, waited for the pianist, the duet, the soprano, the violinist to finish, but still his name was not called.

She remained next to the radio, still in her apron, staring at the speaker as if she might will his voice to come through to her. In the early morning he returned, bareheaded, buttons torn from his shirt, drink on his breath, a gash over one eye.

"Mr. Sloan?" This priest was much younger than the distant figure Ian had met, and shorter, with a warm smile that mocked his somber outfit. Newly ordained, Ian surmised.

"Hello, Father." Seemed odd to address him as "Father."

"I'm sorry I took so long…something came up at the last minute."

"That's all right. We were just watching a movie." He arose from the edge of the bed and stepped toward the door where the priest remained as though reluctant to cross the threshold. Ian knew the old man was watching them, and lowering his voice said, "I don't think he can actually speak much. But he can understand you. His hearing's okay."

"Good. Good. We'll be fine." The paternal manner, uncontrived, was striking in one so young, and Ian felt reassured when the priest touched his forearm and said, "Why don't you get a cup of coffee. We won't be long."

He lingered watching as the priest drew up the chair to the bed and removed a strip of cloth from his bag. He touched the band to his lips and draped it around his neck. The old man followed every movement, mesmerized. The young cleric took his hand and came close to him. The Latin words, unhurried, precise, firm in their embrace. Then he spoke again and the arid lips responded.

The machine at the end of the hall dispensed the muck. He should have known better. Bad coffee was worse than going without, not simply the immediate sense, but the coppery, unwashable.

He sat facing a linen closet and wondering when Pete would arrive. Soon he hoped…if he checked his answering machine. His anger and frustration had, no doubt, come through, but he had no patience for recording messages, certainly not that one. He wanted to reach past the buttons, through the outlet, down the line and grab him by the scruff of the neck…he told him pointedly, ordered him, "Get over here…he won't last long."

A woman in reddish brown hair, a wet coiffure that hung in long, tightly bound strands, sat down on the other end of the bench. She opened her bag and removed a compact and lipstick and began painting, following the red in the trembling mirror, a broad, receptive mouth, incongruous in the pinched face. She wore jeans but the denim lent no substance to the thin legs she kept crossing and recrossing. Wife? Mistress? The latter he decided, banned from the room. The wife in charge now, legality taking precedence.

He turned his attention to the pattern on the tile floor and hoped she would not speak. She probably wouldn't. In hospitals, except for maternity, strangers seldom addressed one another, isolated as they were in their own torment, their own grief. He counted the acoustic squares in the ceiling, one row, then the number of rows, and was multiplying when the priest appeared.

"He's resting comfortably. We communicated perfectly well, no trouble at all. I'm so glad you called." Ian thanked him and couldn't help but think how it might have gone with the other, the older priest. Condescension? Chastisement?… Probably for him too.

His father seemed at ease, almost serene, as he gazed up at the screen. Gyppo was out on the street again, heavy-footed in the darkness, the blood money depleted.

They watched in shared silence, Ian stealing a sideways glance from time to time as he did when he would slip from under the covers and step silently so as not to disturb Pete who had immediately fallen asleep, and creep out to the darkened living room to take up residence on the floor next to his father's armchair. His mother not seeing or pretending not to see.

And there in the dark, with the glow from the ember and the smoke rising purplish in the flickering light, they watched together, the one unaware of the other. And when the old man laughed his congested mirth, a warmth, a sense of well being enveloped Ian.

He stretched his arm along the bed and brushed his father's hand. The touch was disconcerting. With the old man there had never been displays of affection. When they were kids, he never hugged them, never took their hands. They felt his palm only in anger. Their mother did the hugging, the touching. She tried to compensate. She, a seawall against the rage, buffeted in word and deed, more often than not, overwhelmed, but steadfast in her efforts.

She had asked Ian once if he remembered, before Pete was born, how he would latch onto his father's ankle when he returned from work and not let go and the old man would drag him along the floor muttering, *"Jesus-boy-oh-boy...bloody hell."* But the curses would lack their usual vitriol. His spontaneous declaration must have moved his father, though all too quickly forgotten if the old man was awakened untimely from his Sunday nap.

In a short time he no longer embraced the ankle. Older still, and he stepped further back. Soon he learned to keep his distance altogether.

A nurse's aide arrived and began busying herself with trifles, little chores that might be done at any time. She was cheerful and courteous, though, excusing herself when she passed beneath the television to the other side of the bed to tuck in a loose end: "I just love old movies."

Gyppo meandered, collar up, cap low over the eyes. Neither the solitude of the empty street nor the companionship of the bar provided respite. Gyppo could not escape himself.

The camera closed in on the black lettering above the door: Fish and Chips. The news had traveled fast and Gyppo was given a lord's welcome. He hoisted himself atop the counter reveling in their tribute and ordered for all and the stoic watcher bore witness from the other side of the window.

The large vats gave up their smoke and sizzle when the cod dropped into the fryer. And as quickly as they were done, Gyppo distributed the long newspaper cones, steam rising from each, to the outstretched hands, one after another, with generous splashes of the tarty vinegar and sprinkles of salt. A marvelous feast it was and a grand host was Gyppo.

Ian felt a distinct pressure on the wrist. His father's arm had remained stretched across the mattress to where he sat.

Outside, in the cold and damp, the implacable sentry. Soon Gyppo must leave his sanctuary and face the night again. They both had seen the movie before…they knew what was coming…they knew the ending.

The impromptu trial was held in a cavernous cellar, dimly lit, his accusers seated opposite at a long table. Formalities dispensed, the interrogation began in earnest. They had their man but not their confession. Gyppo refused to cooperate. Tormented, confused, alternately acquiescent and belligerent, he deflected their charges to another, denying any involvement, declaring his love for the deceased, for the cause. A puddly anguish. Booze and heartbreak. Seeing it again, Ian realized McLaglen's overacting. Still, he made you care, made you pity Gyppo, overlook his treachery because in a sense Gyppo had done the same. Had never really understood, had gotten caught up in something tragic and did not quite know how.

His father released the pressure and closed his eyes. Ian studied him closely, the breathing still regular.

"Is he sleeping?" Pete was accompanied by the nurse in the gold chain, the attractive one. She stood beside his brother who, in beige slacks and gray linen/silk blend jacket, open neck shirt and sunglasses perched forward on moussed hair, exuded complacency. The clothes, the car, the condo at the beach, he and Britt a temple of chic.

"Just dozed off," said Ian. "We were watching a movie." Pete went slowly to the other side of the bed, measured steps, like a staff sergeant conducting an inspection, and pointed with his thumb at the curtain dividing the room. "Nobody else," said Ian as his brother raised the water pitcher on the nightstand.

"Nurse, can we get some fresh water here…Isn't there something a little cheerier on?" He indicated Gyppo, guilty as charged, locked in a cellar chamber to await his fate.

Pete examined the tubular lines that ran down the old man's arm, then turned his attention to the card, read the inside and was clearly pleased. "Did you talk to the doctor? Are they checking on him regularly? You have to keep after them. I've heard about the neglect in hospitals." His entire manner, each gesture, each word, was meant to convey influence, decisiveness…power. His very silence a declaration.

He had never been in his brother's office, but Ian imagined a gallery. Pete and Britt formal; Pete and Britt casual, the Sloans at play. The camera need only record; they would shoot well in any light. Perhaps it was a good thing they did not have children.

"He came by about an hour ago." Resenting the inquiry and even more the talking over their father as though he were already gone, Ian motioned for his brother to join him in the hall.

"The doctor says he can go at any time. He's not in any pain. He'll just stop breathing."

"Isn't there anything they can do?"

"No…not in his condition."

When they returned, Pete took the chair that belonged to the other bed and placed it next to Ian's.

"Britt has a terrible cold so we didn't think it would be a good idea…you know… spread the germs…she sends her love…well," he said softly, "he's had a long life, when you consider the drinking and smoking and everything."

"True."

"I never thought he'd last this long…anything else on?"

Gyppo had escaped. Mortally wounded, he made his way back to the cathedral, where the old mother remained, bowed in prayer, that timeless symbol of forbearance. Heavenward she dispatched her pleas for her son's almighty soul. Ian remembered many such women in Canada when he was a child. Refugees after the war, Eastern Europeans: Polish, Ukrainians, Czechs, with little or no English. Always kneeling, eyes closed, murmuring in strange tongues. Day or evening one would find a handful scattered among the benches, frail, the black kerchiefs having slipped back to expose the white strands of the heads bowed by private grief and longing.

"This movie's ancient." Pete checked his watch, holding up his wrist for Ian's appreciation. "From Britt, the big 40. Exact time guaranteed. Never be off, not even a second. Should be accurate for what she paid…Have you eaten?"

"Not yet."

"I had a salad. Watching the waistline. How long have you been here?" Ian strained to hear Gyppo's entreaties as he lurched toward the altar, his cap gone, his swaying bulk clutching at the pews as he dragged himself up the aisle. He cried out for the old woman to forgive him. He hadn't meant for it to turn out like this.

"I don't know…couple of hours."

"I would have gotten here sooner but the 405's a complete disaster."

The nurse returned with the water and took her time arranging the table, moving the card, the glass, the card again. She had applied fresh makeup.

"If you need anything, just press the buzzer." She reached across to illustrate, her breasts close to Pete.

"Thank God that's over." The credits rolled. All of them…the entire cast, probably dead now, thought Ian. Had they ever pondered…when they were making the movie…had they ever thought…how much time…how many more days remained? On screen and in memory, the image outlived the man.

"Why don't you take a break…get something to eat. They should have a cafeteria somewhere."

"Yeah, maybe I will. Listen, if he wakes up…if there's any change in his condition get the nurse. Don't wait."

He rode from the sixth to the third floor, the pull of the elevator strangely comforting. Three girls, "Angels," in powder blue pinafores, got on. The area hospitals used them for menial tasks, drawing upon the local high schools for an endless, no-cost supply. Energy, animation, perkiness – prerequisites all. Compassion, kindness, love – extras, nice if you could get them, but certainly not required. A mutually beneficial arrangement it was too. These were the good students, achievers, girls with futures. Girls who understood the value of volunteerism when navigating the intricate world of college admissions.

"Hi, Mr. Sloan." He hadn't looked at them when the doors opened, but instantly recognized the voice, Beverly from his second period honors class. Ambitious, determined, friendly. The other two gazed at him with the amused expression of prior knowledge. Teacher talk would be ready fodder to help cope with the tedium of their voluntary servitude in that depressing realm.

"Hello, Beverly."

"Are you visiting someone?" He felt an immediate aversion to all three and wished to be drippingly sarcastic and tell them he was on tour or conducting research on bedpans or simply enjoyed riding elevators in public places. Even more what he really wanted to tell her was to mind her own business, that the only thing more distasteful than prying was adolescent prying.

"Yes." He did not elaborate and the girl, unaccustomed to reticence, was momentarily stymied, but soon fell back on her good humor. She smiled. They all smiled, a smiling sisterhood. If he were ever confined here, he would leave specific instructions with staff to keep them away

214

from his room. Did hospital windows open? Even death was preferable to their nomadic cheer. He imagined himself pounding futilely on the glass when he heard them coming down the hall.

On the second floor the doors opened to admit a bent figure carrying a walking stick, immaculately dressed in a white, starched shirt and maroon bowtie. Beverly, in dramatic gesture, threw her arm across the door, before exiting. Ian half expected her to start pumping the old guy: "Come to visit or to die?"

"Thank you, dear."

"You're welcome…Mr. Sloan," she called as the door was closing, "DowestillhaveatestonFriday?" He knew she hadn't forgotten but feared she had offended him somehow and wanted to convey that his class was of paramount importance. Gave it her highest priority. A class of significance…after all, she had a grade to protect and would need a recommendation next fall. A quick thinker was Beverly. She would go far.

His companion asked, "Are you a teacher?"

"Yes…" He had paused as if he were admitting a dark secret. "…I am."

"Wonderful. You're so fortunate." He smiled, the thin dyed moustache stretching above the narrow mouth. "Lovely young things, aren't they?"

# TWENTY SIX

He skipped the cafeteria, opting instead for the outdoors and a quick smoke. Inappropriate he surmised, puffing in the entry way, but Sloan didn't really give a damn. Besides, his forlorn presence might very well serve as warning to the addicted, just the deterrent to remind them where they would end up. Eavesdropping twenty years hence he might hear, "Son, I used to smoke when I was your age. I thought I was cool until the time we visited grandma in the hospital and there was this wreck of a guy standing by the door puffing away. He looked so bad I told myself right then and there – no more cigarettes."

He took a long drag, satisfied that, ever the teacher, he would have made a point. What was the cliché'? Even if you get through to only one student, that's reward enough. You are a success. You have done your job. Right,…tell that to the state examiners.

Night, and still they came, relatives, friends, all ages and shapes, some nearer residency than others, filing through the double doors. The obligatory pilgrimage. They would be encouraging, sympathetic, and in their hearts most grateful it was not they on display. The afflicted, in turn, would suffer the collective benignity in stalwart good spirits, yet a repressed envy, resentment even, at the attendees' good health. Initial enthusiasm would wane; in those rooms where minutes became hours, well-wishers, having grown weary of duty's burden, would begin checking their watches, comment, on the lateness of the hour and the need for the patient's rest and he, in turn, gracious in his longing, would forgive them their determination.

A last wave, a smile, a blown kiss. A sigh of relief. Later, perhaps, a stop to eat, a comparing of notes over menus. His face so pale, the drawn, sallow skin, the struggle to speak, the strained syllables, the weak gesture. A time to commiserate, to lift the gloominess from their souls the: the realization that one day they too would await the night alone.

He smoked another cigarette and went inside.


Pete was at the nurses' station and gestured as he might to a subordinate, to wait for instructions. Ian ignored him and hurried to the room.

He remained at the foot of the bed. The body seemed already to have shrunken, to have receded into itself. Mouth open, eyes closed. Had he tried to speak? To cry out? He was grateful he could not see the eyes.

"How is he?"

"Gone...dead." Pete approached the bed, and Ian, eyes fixed on what had been their father, said, "Go tell the nurse."

He sat on the edge of the mattress and placed his palm on the forehead, the skin cold and damp. Where did they go then? Old, gray men with wispy white heads and broken noses and false teeth. Those sad failures who received love they neither deserved nor understood. Might it all come together for them somehow, in some distant place?

He pulled the sheet up around his father's throat just as Pete returned with the nurse in the gold necklace. She checked the vital signs, turned to Pete, closed her eyes and shook her head, in an overly dramatic fashion. Next the doctor, the one who had made the extension offer, to confirm the obvious.

"I'll make the funeral arrangements. I'll take care of everything. Britt can…"

"No funeral. He's being cremated."

"Cremated? I don't think…"

"What?"

"Well,…he was Catholic…I know he didn't go to mass anymore… but, he always… I mean he really believed in…"

"I'm sure he wouldn't mind."


He lay awake in the darkness until well after the buses had ceased running. The last two hurtling past the corner stop outside the apartment around midnight. No one to discharge at that hour.

A collage of scenes, mostly from childhood, but nothing brought him to tears…then the recriminations: he should have remained in the room…returned sooner…he should have been with him…he might have awakened at the end and…and he could have offered…comfort… reassurance …that he might not yet relinquish…his room at the hotel, the Racing Form, the cap, dinner at Everett's, Pepe and the Polack… something profound, heartfelt. A Dylan Thomas invocation. Yet he knew…he understood…the light had been extinguished long before the man.

Near dawn he awakened, eyes moist. He touched the lids with his fingertips and pressed his face into the pillow.

# TWENTY SEVEN

He awoke before the alarm and despite only three hours sleep did not feel tired. He drove the bridge slowly. No rush. He had left early enough, unlike the guy leaning on his horn in the pickup behind. When he came out of the curve, the truck swung around and a twenty-something with cap turned backwards flipped him the finger as he pulled away.

The brilliant sky set afire the long balconies above the arroyo. A pastel blaze, shimmering blues and greens and pinks. This must be what artists meant by "light." He thought he understood now why some painters did the same scene, the same object over and over. If he were an artist, this spectacle would consume him; morning after morning he would render it, thrill to it, in brisk, vivid brushstrokes. At twilight he would luxuriate in the sun's descent, the spilling bronze glow, slow, deep strokes, layered shadings. To give beauty permanence. What better calling?

The freeway to his left a mélange of sight and sound. Another morning, another pursuit. The sun again, but not for his father. And the countless others that had joined him last night. Yet all continued. The room would be cleaned, the ties, the shoes, the cap removed. Would they be given away? To charity? To other tenants? Or tossed into the large trash bin beneath the back stairs. A new resident, a new someone dragging his yesterdays. Gone that rumpled figure dozing before the small black and white tv, an old man, a nobody who boiled coffee in a three-cup aluminum pot on a hotplate, spilling grounds and sugar, leaving rings and taking to his bed to escape a world for which he was ill-suited. Pepe, one or two others, might speak of him for a time, and then no more.

He called Evelyn just before Period 2. She was either out or still in bed, so he left a message telling her he would try again after school. All day he functioned as if encased in a thin membrane, interacting with students, answering questions, giving directions, but his voice distant, outside himself. A few had noticed a change in demeanor, whispered together and stared briefly, but he said nothing. Walking across campus or through the faculty lounge, he paid no heed to the usual chatter. He seemed apart from them, privy to something that made all else irrelevant.

She had just returned from a workout, the gym her refuge she told him when he called later. She could sweat out all her anxiety, her worry, her pain. Last night she had slept soundly for the first time in weeks. Devon had called and said he would be delayed another day. She took Ian's advice and said nothing, no questions, no complaints. He couldn't recall advising such but accepted the tribute. No word from Teddy. She wanted to report him missing, but he urged her to wait one more day. She finally agreed and he told her he would call again in the morning. She had not asked about his father.

He was sitting on the curb, a lonely attendant, guarding the last parking space. When he drew parallel, their eyes met and Ian smiled. Teddy got up, a slow, languid rising.

"Been here long?"

"Not too long." He followed his father up the stairs.

"Can I get a glass of water?"

"Sure, of course…there's milk and I think some juice in the refrigerator. Help yourself."

He put away his books and papers and went into the bedroom to change. In the bathroom he rehearsed what he would say. He wanted to avoid blanket condemnation, but the boy had to realize what his absence had done to his mother.

Teddy was in the wicker chair browsing through an old *Harper's*. "She called you, didn't she?" he said without looking up.

"Yes, of course, she did." He went to the kitchen to put on the kettle. "Do you want some tea?" Silly question. Kids didn't drink tea. Not here, not now. But he had, almost from the time he could remember. The old man loved a strong cup of tea.

"So, where have you been?" Ian slid onto the couch, holding the cup gingerly.

"Around."

"Where's 'around'?" Silence. "Where did you sleep?"

"A friend's garage, but his parents didn't know," Teddy quickly added. "He brought some food out at night." A simple narration, yet in its flatness, a hint of bravado.

"You should have called your mother."

"I did."

"Again."

"Why?"

"To let her know you were okay. We were really worried." A half truth. Ian knew he was fine. "She wanted to report you as a missing person."

"Are you serious?" He dropped the magazine. "That's why I called her in the first place. So she wouldn't do anything dumb…call the cops or anything."

"Teddy, that was three days ago." His son emitted a hiss, echoes of Blaine Wexler and all the other self-absorbed Blaines, for whom acting on impulse and gratifying desire were native claims. Had his own kid become one of them? "Listen, Teddy…" He retreated. He had not earned the right to scold. And his son had come to him, not to his mother. "Are you hungry?"

"Yeah, a little."

"Let's get something to eat."

"I like your apartment." He contemplated the room as if he were making calculations.

"You've been here before."

"Only a couple of times…kind of forgot what it looked like. It looks different…It's got…character."

They walked to a neighborhood restaurant, a simple coffee shop, simple food: hamburger steak, pot roast, pork chops, a menu from a time when pasta was simply spaghetti and inexpensive. No California cuisine then. Everett's, where the old man ate, was a similar relic. Now the local place was more apt to be Thai, Vietnamese, Indian, or the ubiquitous Mexican or Chinese. And even Everett's was adapting, purple neon in the window, a royal script announcing "cappuccino." What the hell was "cappuccino" his father had wanted to know.

Formica counter, vinyl booths and the glass with the slanted mirror reflecting the swirl capped pies. They took a corner booth next to a window with grimy venetian blinds and said little yet comfortable with one another.

Teddy plowed his way through chicken fried steak, shoestring potatoes, salad, and dessert. Ian watched him, intent on his food, eating with the hunger of youth, mechanical, direct, purposeful. They had not sat down regularly to a meal since Teddy was a child and now he was almost a man. Pale like him when he was a teenager with long, white bony arms and slender hands. Evelyn was darker, more pigmented, her skin seemed to adapt to the elements. Teddy had inherited his coloring, or lack of it but…she had always been there. He should have been more

224

a witness to his son's development, to the shedding of childhood. He might have helped with the transition.

Lost time. Lost opportunity. Not a meeting one reconvened at convenience, picking up where they left off.

"Dad, are you all right?"

"Yes, fine. Just watching you eat."

"Okayyy." Teddy rolled his eyes, his face flushed, embarrassed but pleased.

"I thought you were only 'a little' hungry," said Ian when they were outside.

"More than I thought."

"Ever see Jasmine again?"

They walked slowly, the stroll of digestion. So much he wanted to know; however, like trying to join a conversation in progress, Ian was uncertain how to proceed.

"No, she's an airhead."

"She might be very nice, once you get to know her."

"Nah, she's an airhead."

"Good looking, though. You should give her a call some time."

He could not conceive of the old man ever talking to him like this. The mere hint of sex was verboten, more weakness than shared pleasure, succumb to in the dark without comment, though once he had heard late at night: "…my bloody right…your duty…a good wife… can't refuse her husband…"

They continued, speaking little, until Ian realized that without consciously doing so, he was leading them toward the bridge.

"Getting tired?" Teddy had slowed.

"Where are we going?"

"To the bridge…but if you're tired…"

"If you can make it, so can I."

"You'd better be able to. I've got about thirty years on you."

# TWENTY EIGHT

His initial burst had quickly faded and given way to a dogged determination to keep abreast of Teddy, who seemed to grow stronger as they ascended. When they reached the summit, Ian collapsed against the railing. "I'm beat. Let's rest awhile."

"It's called 'Suicide Bridge,'" said Teddy. They sat on the stone bench in the first nook.

"I've heard that."

"There's a plaque at our school for a kid who was killed here in the Fifties."

"What happened?"

"He was hit by a car. He was riding his bike. When I was a freshman, one of our teachers told us. The driver was speeding. And this kid was a really good student. Smart. Student government. Popular. Big jock – everything. There's a patio named after him too."

"Speaking of school. I hope you haven't fallen too far behind."

"I can catch up. The work's not that hard."

They had just resumed their hike when a convertible appeared from the opposite direction, two girls, the radio blaring, and from the passenger side, "Hey, Babe!"

Teddy ignored them and Ian turned an appraising eye. They were about the same height but he felt sure Teddy would continue to grow. He was good looking, not simply adolescent cuteness. The pensive expression suggested maturity, handsomeness. Soon, Ian knew, if not already, women would take notice.

"What did you do all day?"

"Went to the library, the park."

"Didn't anyone ask you why you weren't in school?"

"One of the librarians. But I told her I was a college student and we were out already."

"Why did you take off like that? Your mother thought things were going better."

"I tried to be the good little boy so she would think everything was cool. But I just couldn't take it anymore. I don't know…I can't explain it. I just wanted to get out of there. Didn't you ever feel like you wanted to get away?" He no longer sounded seventeen.

"Sure." They had reached the end and crossed over for the return trip. "Actually, I have been away."

"What do you mean?"

"Away from you. The absent father. Here am I critical of other kids' parents and I'm guilty too."

"But you and Mom…she's got Devon…I understand if you didn't want to come around much."

"If I hadn't been so wrapped up in myself…I would have realized what I was missing. I suppose in a way I abandoned you. And you know what the worst part is? I rarely felt guilty. I was so…"

"Dad,…you don't have to explain. I…"

"Seeing you sitting there waiting for me, I realized what a bastard I've been."

They walked on, in and out of darkness, illuminated at intervals as they passed beneath the lamps.

"Do you like teaching?"

"Yes and no…Why?

"I don't know…sometimes when I look at the teachers at my school, I think it's a rotten job. All the stuff that goes on. But then sometimes it doesn't seem so bad. Did your parents want you to be a teacher?"

"No, no." He laughed and shook his head. How could he explain a time when most parents did not expect their kid to go to college. His certainly didn't. His own students had no sense of yesteryear, no knowledge unless the period was relevant. The past, if not utilitarian – translation: a test question – had no value. They had a better grasp of the Roman Empire than they did of Watergate. "They never had plans… not for Pete and me, not for themselves. The future for my mother was usually immediate. She couldn't always count on Grandpa. And he didn't care what I did as long as I stayed out of trouble. For him a good education was a high school diploma. He never finished elementary school."

"Really?"

"He went to work in the Glasgow shipyards. A different world then, Teddy. All you needed was a trade, a skill, and you could make a decent living…if you worked."

"Why did you become a teacher then?"

"I'm not exactly sure. I had worked in the business world – low level positions. It all just seemed so tedious and meaningless…and I had always enjoyed literature. I suppose the idea of getting paid to talk about it seemed a good deal."

"Mom told me Grandpa wasn't a good father…that he beat you and Uncle Pete and got drunk all the time."

"Let's rest for a minute." They sat again in one of the alcoves.

"Some men don't make good fathers, Teddy…huh, look who's talking."

"You're not an alcoholic…and you never…"

"I mean they shouldn't have children, probably shouldn't even marry and if they do, they need a strong woman, a woman that will stand up to them. Keep them in line. Your grandma wasn't like that… oh, she was strong, very strong, in other ways…if it wasn't for her there were times when we wouldn't have had food on the table. And she would defend us…and take a lot from him. But with a man like grandpa you needed more than pleading. She needed to…give him an ultimatum and you had to do it early. The longer she waited, the harder it would become. After I was born and especially after your Uncle Pete, it was too late.

Your mother's not strong either…but in a different way."

"What way?"

"Well…insecure, I guess…uncertain…She's always afraid she's missing out on something, something that will make her happy…happier." They were sitting shoulder to shoulder. "Teddy?"

"Yes," he answered vacantly, lost to the moment, his heel tracing crescents on the concrete.

"Grandpa's been sick. He was in the hospital for a couple of weeks."

"Mom told me."

"You know…he was in pretty bad shape, getting weaker and weaker and…"

"He died?"

"Last night, in his sleep. He didn't suffer at all."

"I didn't get to see him…I should have visited…" His chest heaved, a sharp intake, and Ian put his arm around him.

"He was going in and out of consciousness…he couldn't recognize anyone…Grandpa knew you loved him…and he loved you."

"I want to come and stay with you." He continued staring at his feet, the softness of his voice nearly lost in the rattling of a dilapidated truck, wood slats corralling a mountain of shifting debris and scrawled in crooked red letters on a piece of dangling plywood: "Cyril's Trash Removal."

"Teddy, I'd love to have you but… it's not possible, not now."

"Why?"

"Your place is with your mother. Anyway, my apartment's too small."

"I can sleep on the couch."

"Your mother needs you. Especially now."

"Why? What's the matter?"

"She's going through a bit of a hard time…with Devon. And she's really been worried about you. If you came to live with me, I think she'd feel betrayed."

"She doesn't need me."

"She does. She needs your support. Besides, there's not enough room at my place. We'd get in each other's way. Only one bathroom and…there's no pool. It's cramped. You're used to a lot of room. I don't think it would be very comfortable for you."

"Sure it would…I don't care about a pool."

"You only have a year to go and then you'll be off to college."

"I might not go to college…at least not right away."

"You can work then. Maybe get your own apartment if you want… in fact, I'm thinking of moving myself."

"You are? Where?"

"I'm not sure…not far. A better place."

"Are you getting married or something?"

"No, no," he laughed. "I think I'm beyond that, for the time being anyway."

"Do you have a…are you seeing anyone?"

"Teddy, at my age it's not so easy…"

"You're not that old. My friend Will, his parents are divorced and his father has a girlfriend. I think he's older than you."

"I wouldn't know how to get started."

"You could rent a two-bedroom apartment or a house. Then we'd have lots of room."

"Listen, I want you to go back to your mother. Work hard to get caught up and do well on your finals and I'll talk to your mother and if she agrees, you can come and stay with me from time to time. How's that sound?"

"I guess…"

"And you know what? I think I'm going to get a new car. It's time to dump the Rabbit."

"Dad! New apartment? New car?"

"I've been in a rut. Time to break out…any idea what I should get?"

"Get something really nice…something sporty."

"Want to go looking with me."

"Yeah, sure."

The descent was much less demanding. Teddy was ebullient, grinning, laughing, sentences left dangling, starting anew, grabbing a thought here an observation there, as one might cram a bag, the taxi waiting below. And Ian, the joyous companion, along for the ride.

Her reaction was just as he had expected – hurt, disappointment, implied blame. After a brief exchange he put Teddy on the line. He said little, only the occasional "yes" or "no," the fingers of his free hand as though wishing to participate in the conversation moving across the table and in and out of his pocket. Afterwards, he told Ian she had cried and asked where she had gone wrong and did he still love her.

They stayed late watching television and talking. About the past, about the future. About what kind of car he should get. Nothing dull, Teddy insisted. No Buicks, no Chryslers.

Around four he got up for the bathroom and checked on the body turned sideways, too long for the couch, but breathing easily.

# TWENTY NINE

The last issue. They would go to press tomorrow and come out on Friday, but this was no ordinary deadline day. The banter was more subdued, less frenzied, no annoyance, the humor a conscious staging. Conversations tinged with nostalgia as each began to comprehend the immutability of "last." And on Friday, this final issue distributed, they would surrender to reminiscence. Laugh at bungled headlines, incorrect photo ids, ads with expired discounts, all the difficulties and minor crises that had driven some to near homicide, or at the very least, acrimonious exchanges and deadly silence that stretched into days, weeks even. All the pain and frustration would be lost now in a communal wistfulness. For seniors on staff, a dress rehearsal for what awaited on graduation day.

And with the laughter, the promises, the sad joy, a profound longing to bottle these final days, in which even the most jaded, the most experienced, felt new again, to take with them and uncork at their leisure. Then by late July the backward glances would have turned forward to travel arrangements and packing and dorms and a growing sense of expectation, apprehension. But for now and for most —tears. Sloan, veteran high priest of this June rite, wondered whether Julie would finally allow herself that one indulgence.

"He was never available, Mr. Sloan. I know he was avoiding me. But we have to decide, we can't wait any longer." He appreciated the "we," not that he was hearing it for the first time. For Julie, the *Roar* was always plural, though in in fact, it was "she" more than the others combined. But to be joined with her, that once timid freshman who wouldn't look him in the eye that first September, was, he realized, important to him.

"Did you get the numbers from the other schools?"

"I went to four and called eight others, but nobody would tell me anything. They were nice but they said they couldn't give out that information but..." She paused for effect. "I got ours." A triumphant grin. No smugness. Simply exultation..

"How?"

"I started going back through the minutes of every Board meeting for the last two years. I found it in October '85 - $14,000."

"Of course! I never thought...good work."

"But, Mr. Sloan, what can we do with it? We don't have anything to compare it to."

"Doesn't matter. Go ahead and write the editorial. Give the figure and state you had to find the information yourself. You got no cooperation from the district office. Don't make any accusations. All you're doing is raising the question as to why there was no bidding on the contract. Just lay out the facts as you know them." She was delighted. This would be more than the usual year-end Senior Salute issue.

"I wish I could be here to do a follow-up."

"The main thing is you raised the issue. Informed the readers."

"Mr. Sloan," she edged toward his desk, the freshman reincarnated, clutching the yellow pad, struggling, "I want to tell you...I mean... I don't know how..."

"You better get to work on the editorial. You…We don't have much time." He busied himself searching for a non-existent folder, and the editor-in-chief remained in place, perfectly still, until duty finally took precedence and without further word strode away.

He watched her navigating among the mélange of legs and elbows and back-packs to ask and answer questions and wished that Teddy knew her.

Some of the staff had already left, but most were still on campus, in their rooms or the faculty lounge, when the announcement came over the p.a. system. An emergency meeting in the library in five minutes. Speculation ran high. An accident? A death? Milton in foreign languages? Only 48 and bypass surgery last year.

Something bleak, thought Sloan; emergency confabs were rarely otherwise. Good news could always wait.

"What's going on?"

"No idea. I just obey The Man." Roth was hunched over the *Times* crossword, his whiskers stroking the clues.

"Jesus, if you were any closer you'd be wearing the letters…ever think of getting new glasses?"

"Concentration. It's all about the concentration."

Milton was still upright, in private conversation with Vivian Shelby, perhaps discussing the Grand Dame's itinerary: England, France, Italy, Austria, Germany. Except for Greece, of course, the Balkans held little interest. Eastern Europe drab as an old trench coat. Scandinavia might warrant a nod, but Keats, Shelley, the Empire that once was, afternoon tea and the British Museum - her true destination. Eventually she would make her way south, the Mediterranean, a palette's blue, olive and citrus and jasmine: a scented musing.

But for fate, this sojourn of Vivian's essential self, this province of her heart, might well have been her residence, not merely her refuge.

Indeed, she had often sensed a part of her lay interred on that much loved island.

This summer, though, she would linger into an autumn indulgence: afternoon strolls beneath the elm and chestnut trees, coats buttoned against the October chill. London, Paris, a late Fall charm all their own.

All was in the timing. With the recent changes in curriculum, the elevating of contemporary literature, the trumpeting of diversity, the ethnic cannon – all sadly misguided ventures she feared – yes, her time had come. Like Arthur drifting downstream, Anesthesia, her Camelot, would recede into the mist.

At 3:49 "The Great Dane." A resolute arrival. He ignored the buzz of the moment and took position by the entrance, spread-eagle, feet planted firmly beneath the Anesthesia seal: Courage, Integrity, Fellowship, Compassion.

"What's a five-letter word for 'termination,'" mumbled Roth.

"Thank you for coming," said Bengstrom in the officer's cadence. Even at Waterloo, Napoleon was still Napoleon. "I'm sorry for the late notice but it could not be helped. I have an announcement to make. I want you to hear it from me personally…so you have it straight from the horse's mouth." The lower lip quivered and Napoleon went up an octave. "I will not be returning as your principal next year." Louise Randall gasped, a pause and then the deluge.

A mob of feigned commiseration and outrage, wanting details, wanting names, wanting enough to nourish communal tables at brunch and lunch for at least the next week. A torrent that seemed for an instant to overwhelm the general but he held his ground.

"Please, please…I appreciate your concern…I just want you to know that no one is tying a can to my tail."

"Still in denial," said Sloan, yet he almost felt a respect for Bengstrom's holding himself together, a wounded dignity and Malcom's

236

summation at Cawdor's execution came to mind: "Nothing In his life became him/Like the leaving of it."

The principal turned abruptly and collided with Wendy Gibbons, Special Ed. who, though eighteen, looked twelve in her frock and braids. She had a childlike directness that allowed for access to anyone at anytime, once demanding of Thurman, who was installing plastic liners in the trash barrels and had recently learned from Readers Digest that memory loss was an early indication of dotage, the name of the third President, causing the custodian much consternation as it was just on the tip of his tongue.

"Mr. Bengstrom," she called, at the heels of the about-to-be former principal, "Mr. Bengstrom, Mr. Bengstrom...How do you spell 'skool'?"

# THIRTY

Bengstrom's farewell left him behind schedule. A leisurely shower and change of clothes before meeting Teddy seemed remote. He let up on the accelerator; a ticket now would really delay him.

He was to pick up Teddy around five, allowing them plenty of time to get something to eat before the game, the first of three with the rival Giants. They would go to a place on Sunset not far from the stadium. A hole-in-the-wall that had been there forever, already well established when he arrived in L.A.. His first taste of Mexican food. Teddy had said his apartment had "atmosphere," so he would no doubt find the dive interesting.

At a red light he thought of Bengstrom. He saw again the principal blustering out from behind his desk, hitching up his pants, drawing in his jacket, prepared for action, prepared to take steps...prepared for nothing. "The Great Dane." Penned. Neutered. His career effectively over. At his age another principal ship doubtful, and despite the current rhetoric extolling the virtues of teaching, the idea of actually returning to the classroom was abhorrent to most administrators. Not just the salary cut, but more the loss of position, of status. A step backward. A failure. A loser. So much for the noble calling.

A black Mercedes sedan swept across the intersection in a wide, luxurious turn. All was in the winning mused Ian, work, play, grades, appearance… Everything. But teaching was non competitive, at least not meant to be. No bonuses. No promotions. No one-up-man-ships. No victors. Nothing to flaunt: completely un-American.

The prospect of the evening ahead invigorated him; he felt none of the usual late afternoon fatigue. They were beginning to be more comfortable with each other, almost as though they had never been apart.

He would remain. He would keep the *Roar* true to Julie's spirit. He had no choice. She would be monitoring them from afar. A new principal. One less paranoid he hoped. Though in Bengstrom's case they were out to get him. On the other hand, paranoia might very well be endemic to the position, a prerequisite: Wanted – educator with persecution complex, adept at furtive glances and uncovering plots. Didn't really matter to Sloan. He would cope, might even take his turn as Chair.

He approached the turnoff for the bridge and the freeway and, with a quick look backward, swung into the right lane at the last minute and negotiated the freeway on ramp.

The traffic was heavy. Sloan eased into the train of cars and maneuvered across lanes to the inside to make up for lost time.